Anything That You Want

A Sweet Romantic Comedy

Mary Carson

Inconceivable Press

Cover Design by Sarah Kil Creative Studio

Proofreading by LaLinc

Sensitivity Read by TM

To Susan Kostelecky
You were with me every word of the way. Literally.
I couldn't have done it without you, Dude.

To My Dad, the Best Dad
and the Original Daddio
Thank you for catching what is now formally known as the
Bunk Bed Plot Hole.
It's a much richer story because of you!

To My Mom, the Best Mom
You kept saying you don't like romance but were the first to
ask
how it was going, and what was going to happen next.
I'm on to you, Mom.
P.S. Your prune kolaches are still the best!

And to Mr. Carson
Who is more perfect than even James.

Contents

Keep In Touch

I'd love to hear from you!

Keep in touch through my newsletter, where we talk about all things books...and then even more things books!

Get bookish email right in your inbox – join me here – www.marycarsonbooks.com/about

Note From The Author

Dear Reader,

Though this book is sweet, funny, and heartwarming, there are some sensitive subjects involved. There is discussion of estranged and deserted family members, mention of negative foster care experiences, mention of family members who have lost their lives to drug addiction, and discussion of adoption.

I'd like to extend a special thank you to T McG for serving as my sensitivity reader to ensure that Ellie and her family have been represented with care and accuracy. Any misrepresentation is entirely my own.

Wishing you well,
-Mary

Chapter 1

- *Ellie*

My eyes darted around the ballroom, searching for something, *anything*, that might save me. The room, filled with rich people dripping in diamonds and pearls, had turned into my own, personal, *escape room* hell. I was trapped. Here. At the annual Merit Memorial Hospital Charity Ball, where the charity was an afterthought, and being seen was the real reason for the evening.

I did another scan around, and almost sighed aloud when I spotted my one true friend, Jasmine, approaching with two tall glasses of champagne.

"Here. Take this." Jasmine pressed a drink into my hand. "You look like you need it."

"Oh, I most definitely do, but I can't. I'm on-call tonight. Quick, say something to make me laugh."

"You mean something like—when I got dressed tonight my goal was to out-sparkle the crystal chandeliers." Handing me both drinks, she did a little spin, so I could see she had come admirably close to her goal.

"You're like a teeny, tiny disco ball in all that bling. I think the chandeliers are jealous."

"Thank you, my dear, mission accomplished. My mother always said 'don't hide your light under a bushel.' I took those words seriously."

"And it is clear you do."

Jasmine looked incredible in a crystal-studded bustier pantsuit, which she finished off with strappy sky-high stilettos. She was the only person I knew who could get away with pants at a black-tie affair. She had so much confidence.

Handing the drinks back, I glanced around the room. "I'm actually hoping to get called in. Anything to get away from these rich snobs, and get away from Marks." I looked over at my colleague, the never-not-butt-kissing Dr. John Marks, currently in the throes of Department Head adulation. I wanted to kick him in the shins.

Jasmine smirked, "Marks. Such a D."

"He is." I tried to take a big breath, then fought the urge to squirm. "Jas, I've got to get out of this dress. My strapless bra is so tight, I might need oxygen before the night is over." My dress felt like a straight jacket, testing both my lungs and my sanity.

Jasmine laughed her fabulous laugh, then proceeded to take a big drink of champagne. Unlike me, she could see the humor in almost any situation. I had no idea how to do that.

"One, I'll go ahead and drink both of these, thank you very much. Two, that strapless bra is doing wonders for your girls, so work it while you can. Maybe your wish to get out of that dress will come true. If you know what I mean." She raised her eyebrows up and down at that, and I rolled my eyes.

"And three, how many times do we have to talk about this, Ellie? There is nothing that Dr. Marks can say or do to negate the fact that you are the front runner for the hospital's Tate Award. Can't you just enjoy him for his looks? There are definitely less attractive and more annoying men you could've ended up hanging with here tonight."

I shook my head in disagreement. "Enjoy him for his looks? I can't see past all the puckering he's doing to even get to his looks. Know what he said earlier tonight? That I'll never win the Tate with my 'lone wolf' attitude. That I need to be more of a 'team player.' As if. He even used air quotes when he said it."

Jasmine started to reply when raised voices drew our attention.

Other than hospital staff, I didn't know anyone there. Who had time for socializing, especially with that type of crowd, the upper crust crowd of charity event attendees? Merit wasn't the biggest city in North Carolina, but it was big enough, and everyone there thought they were sooo important. Just ask them. But then I saw the guy causing the commotion. I had a fleeting wish I'd expanded my social circle if it meant it was going to include him.

He was tall, much taller than my 5'10", even in my heels, and that didn't happen very often. Broad in the shoulders, too, and it was clear his tux was made just for him. He had sun-streaked brown hair that was falling in his eyes, and a tan complexion, like he did a lot of work outdoors—or played a lot of golf.

I snorted to myself. Of course he played a lot of golf. Rich jerk.

Jasmine arched her left eyebrow and gave me a look like—get a load of these two.

The man patted himself down, obviously searching for something. His wallet? His phone? The beautiful woman next to him frowned and shook her head, frustration written all over her pretty face.

"James. It's the first night we've been out in weeks and you promised you would leave work behind. Don't answer that phone," said the brunette beauty.

I shot a look at Jasmine. James shouldn't make promises to his girlfriend he's not willing to keep.

James found his phone, glanced at it, and cursed under his breath. "I've got to go." He came dashing by and bumped right into Jasmine. And those two drinks in her hands? Now they were all over me. My dress. And my cleavage. Lovely.

The guy raced past and barely glanced in our direction. "Sorry," he called and ran straight out of the ballroom. The room practically went silent, and all eyes followed him.

Jasmine and I were in shock. Maybe in even more shock than his girlfriend, who stood there with her mouth open. Jilted.

The noise of the crowd grew. People burst into animated conversation, speculating over what had happened.

Jasmine reacted before I did, and placed the now empty champagne flutes onto a nearby table. "Ladies' room. STAT." She grabbed my hand and pulled me toward the front of the room. The two of us created our own little scene, pushing through the guests.

"I'll get you another drink," I heard behind me. The ever-helpful Dr. Marks. Like that was going to make everything better. I'm on-call, remember? I didn't even have a drink.

Wait. Let me restate. I did have a drink.

All over me.

"Holy frijoles, girl, I can't believe that guy ran into us and didn't even stop." Jasmine slammed our way into the ladies' room and made a beeline for the paper towel dispenser. I positioned myself at the sink, and she fast-fired the towels to me. I dabbed at my gown and attempted to lessen the damage. We were good in a crisis—even a dress crisis.

"I thought tonight's entertainment was going to be that rich jerk James and his girlfriend having an argument." I continued to wipe at my dress, hoping for a miracle. "I didn't suspect for a second that I was going to become the show."

"Well, I told you your girls looked good in that bra. You were going to become a show somehow tonight." She grinned and threw me another paper towel.

I grinned back and lobbed a soaking-wet, scrunched-up towel right past her head.

Jasmine laughed, reached down and picked up the wet mess, and threw it in the trash. She gave me a curious glance. "You looked at him more than once, you know. A lot more."

"Nope," I was quick to reply. Maybe a little too quick? "Just the once was plenty. I need a rude, rich dude like I need a hole in the head. You know the Tate Award is all that I care about." James might have been attractive—okay, really attractive—but now he was the guy without manners who spilled drinks all over without remorse, and ditched his girl without a goodbye. Figures.

"All right." Jasmine walked over to where I stood. "Let's see what we're working with."

We both stood in front of the mirror, side by side, and took in the disaster.

"Good news," I said.

Jasmine cocked her head. "Is there, though?"

"Yep. I've got scrubs in the car. And I can use this as an excuse to leave this stupid party. And Dr. Marks."

At that moment, my hospital on-call ringtone went off.

Chapter 2

- *Ellie*

"Duty calls!" I grinned from ear to ear at Jasmine, then replied to the page that I was on my way.

"You lucky dog. You did it—you're getting out of here. With a legit excuse, no less."

"I'm not so sure about the 'lucky' part—I am covered in booze. I'll just change at the hospital. Thanks so much for your help, Jas. I'll catch you later." I leaned in and gave Jas a quick hug.

"Go, go," she said. "Be safe on your drive."

I raced towards the hotel lobby, thoughts of good-looking men who were beyond rude pushed to the back of my mind. I had less than fifteen minutes to get to the hospital, get changed, and assess the situation. The main reason the charity ball was held at this hotel was because it was so close to the hospital, specifically in case some member of the staff needed to get there fast.

I bypassed the elevators and dashed down the gilded sweeping staircase from the Ballroom to the Lobby. Because I was on-call, I'd asked the valet to park my car in the nearby VIP section—for just this situation. Sometimes being a doctor had its perks.

I rushed up to the valet.

His eyes went wide, startled.

No, it wasn't due to the speed of my approach, rather, it was the state of my dress. Shoot. I'd already forgotten.

"Hurry—I'm on-call at the hospital. I need my car right away. It's VIP #3." I snagged the valet stub from my tiny evening bag and handed it to the young man.

"Yes, ma'am. Right away ma'am." He nodded his head and turned to the valet stand of keys and halted. He turned back to me, then turned back to the stand.

"What is it?" My words were rushed.

He turned and held his hands up.

"Um, ma'am. Your car keys are not here."

"What?" I asked. Or maybe shrieked. And when did I become a "ma'am"? Surely I'm still a "miss"? No—I'm a doctor! "That makes no sense whatsoever. Maybe it's just on the wrong hook. It has a large blue and white Merit Memorial Hospital medallion on it."

I darted around the valet stand and searched through the keys. Well, shoot. There were a ton of Merit Hospital keychains since it was our charity event being hosted. But still, it was clear to me within seconds. My keys weren't there. For the second time tonight, I froze.

I shook myself out of it and took a few quick steps toward the entrance. I looked out the floor-to-ceiling glass windows, and there was my proof. The #3 spot in VIP parking was empty. *What. The. What?*

My mind spun. It wasn't as if I had gone into the night thinking the charity event would turn into some kind of fairy tale ball, complete with a Prince Charming and a fairy godmother. But when I put on my beautiful dress and tried not to put too much hope into the possibility of the night, not once did I think the evening would end with me covered in champagne and my car stolen. Not. Once.

I turned back toward the valet. "It's gone. My car is just gone. Where is my car?"

The valet's eyes were bigger than ever. He'd probably never been in this position before, but I didn't have a lot of empathy at the moment. His gaze went everywhere, but the rest of his body stood there, doing nothing.

"I've got to get to the hospital. Now!"

It was my very loud exclamation that got what appeared to be the hotel manager striding over to the valet stand.

"Ma'am. Is there something I can help you with?"

Again with the "ma'am"? Nobody has time for this, especially me. I inhaled slowly, then proceeded calmly and patiently, like I would in any emergency.

I moved to the front doors and thanked God for the proximity of the hotel to the hospital.

"I'm Dr. Dumont and I was just called into the hospital. My silver Lexus is missing. Find my car."

The manager's eyebrows reached for her hairline. It was almost comical. "*Wait.* There must be—"

I kind of wished I could stick around to see what happened next, but I was already power walking out the door and into the cool night air. I didn't have on the best shoes for this trek to the hospital, but I'd make it.

Getting an emergency page was exciting. When I set up my fertility clinic in partnership with the hospital, part of the deal was that I would take on-call shifts. That was fine by me—I loved my work.

I dialed the charge nurse's station.

"Shannon. It's Dr. Dumont. I'm four minutes out. I need you to open my locker and pull out my tennis shoes and a set of scrubs. And just leave the locker open. What's the status of the patient?"

Shannon filled me in. The patient was a 32-year-old woman, laboring for the first time. She was one week early and had gestational diabetes. Her OB doctor would typically handle the delivery, but she was too far along for her doctor to get in. Because of her diabetes, they wanted someone now, and I was the OB doc on service. I was always glad when they called me in. It was better for everyone if, for some reason, the quick delivery took a turn that no one was expecting.

I rushed into the ER and Shannon called out from the nursing station.

"Dr. Dumont! You're in room 2. Your shoes and scrubs are waiting."

I gave Shannon a wave and pushed my way into the locker room. I discarded my heels and dress and pulled on my scrubs and running shoes. Sweet relief. Not just because I was out of the liquor-soaked dress, but because this was home to me. In my uniform. In my hospital. I fit here.

I took in a deep breath, slowly blew it out, then stepped into the patient's room. Glancing at her chart, I grabbed some gloves and sat down on a rolling stool. I slid over to my patient, who panted and breathed heavily. I blocked out everyone in the room, focused solely on my patient, and gave her a reassuring smile.

"Elizabeth, I'm Dr. Dumont. I'm here in place of your doctor because things are happening fast. Hang on while I just take a look." I did a quick cervical check and saw that she was fully dilated and ready to push.

"Looks like you're ready, Elizabeth. We're way past the time for an epidural, so let's get you onto your hands and knees. It'll be more comfortable for you."

I glanced at Nurse Judy. "Call L and D and let them know we're delivering here."

Soon the baby crowned, and in no time the labor was complete. I was relieved to see that despite diabetes, the baby was a perfect size.

"Congratulations," I said, "You have a beautiful baby boy."

Nurse Judy settled the baby on Elizabeth's chest, then gently wiped him down.

Tears ran down Elizabeth's cheeks. She glanced at me, then back to the baby, and laughed. "Why does he smell so good?"

I smiled, then pushed away from Elizabeth to dispose of my gloves and wash my hands. I heard Elizabeth and her husband *ooh* and *ah*, making soft exclaims of delight. I turned from the sink to address the happy couple.

"So have you picked out any names yet?"

Whoever said 'the third time is the charm' had no idea what they were talking about. Because for the third time that night, I froze. Standing next to Elizabeth, looking down lovingly at his brand new baby boy, was *James*.

Chapter 3

- *Ellie*

What was going on?

This was the exact same guy from the charity ball, right? The one who ran into Jasmine, causing her to dump drinks all over me while he ran out the door with no apology?

My confusion was cleared up pretty quickly by the fact that yes, he stood there in a tux shirt and pants while the woman who just gave birth to his baby lovingly said, "James, look at how perfect he is," while she simultaneously placed James's hand on the baby's back.

Unbelievable. Less than an hour ago he was at the ball with another woman while his wife? Girlfriend? Mistress? Baby mama? Was about to give birth. And for one second I'd thought he was hot. For the first time in I don't know how long, no matter how much I denied it to Jasmine, I'd found myself thinking a guy was attractive and allowed myself to daydream about what-ifs, and he was this fine specimen of morality? No. Just no. Another great example of why I was better off on my own.

Elizabeth looked up at me.

"We haven't settled on a name, Doctor, but I've always thought James was a good strong name. Perfect for growing into a good strong man." She beamed at James.

He glanced at Elizabeth. "Lizzy, you know I'd love that," he said and reached for her hand.

It was perfectly clear that James had no idea that I was the woman he dumped champagne all over. He probably had a hard time keeping all of the women in his life straight, what with the way he bounced around between them. Okay. Enough of this. That man—who barely knew I existed—had taken up way too much of my mind tonight. It was time to get out of here.

"Congratulations to you both. Nurse Judy will make sure you have everything you need, and your personal obstetrician will contact you to make an appointment for the first of the week. I'll get all of the notes to him first thing, letting him know everything went smoothly, with no complications. Enjoy your night, and get some rest while you can."

With that, I turned and walked out.

I came to with a start. I wasn't surprised that I woke up on my desk again. It happened a lot more often than it should. I had decided to stick around the hospital, since I was still on-call, and needed to finish up my notes on Elizabeth's delivery. One hour turned into two, and when I put my head down on the desk "just for a minute," it turned into a lot more than a minute.

The sun was coming in through the window, so it was later than I thought. All I wanted at this point was a hot bath and my bed. My on-call shift ended about two hours ago, so I would close out my notes, jump in my car, and .... Shoot. My car. How did I forget about my car?

I grabbed my phone and wondered who I should call first when I saw a text from Jasmine.

Jas: *Hey girl. Just checking in. The ball ended...well not with a bang but with a fizzle. You didn't miss a thing. How'd on-call end up?*

Me: You won't even believe. But I'm in a rush. Let's talk later.

Jas: *Girl! Cryptic much? Don't leave me hanging!*

Me: Talk Monday! :)

I really didn't have time to get into everything with Jasmine because I had to get my car back. Besides, she knew me well. She knew I was much more likely to talk when we were face-to-face.

I decided not to call the police until I talked to the hotel, so I searched for the number and called.

"Thank you for calling the Luxor Hotel, where you always feel at home. This is Chad, how may I be of service?" The man sounded super upbeat. I wondered how long he would sound that way once he knew I was the woman with the stolen car calling.

"Hello, this is Dr. Eleanor Dumont. Last night my car—"

"Ms. Dumont. Oh, we are so glad you called. We—"

"It's Dr. Dumont. " I'm positive if Dr. Marks had called, Chad would have called him doctor.

Chad continued in his upbeat manner.

"Of course, of course, Dr. Dumont. We didn't have your number and hadn't been able to track anyone down from the charity ball to get your contact information, but we have great news!"

Great news? That was the last thing I expected.

"You do?"

"Yes. We have your car. I mean, we don't have your car, we know where your car is. It's at the hospital."

Chad was super pleased to share this information with me. At the hospital? That couldn't be right.

"What? I'm at the hospital. What do you mean my car is at the hospital?"

Chad filled me in, and he barely took a breath to get it all out.

"Late last night a man called and said he'd had an emergency earlier in the evening and 'borrowed' a car from VIP by grabbing a key from valet while our employees were with other guests. We are so sorry this happened, Dr. Dumont, and I can assure you we will be revisiting our valet procedures to ensure nothing like this happens again."

I couldn't care less about their valet procedures, what about my car?

"And my car is...?"

"He left the keys under your floor mat and your car is parked in the Emergency Parking lot."

Huh. I did not see that coming. Suddenly, everything about my day looked better. I thought I would be spending hours trying to track down my car, knowing there was a distinct possibility I might never get it back, and instead I'd be able to just walk out of the hospital. Fancy that.

"Well, Chad, you've surprised me. Lucky for you, I'm exhausted. So assuming there is nothing wrong with my car, this will be the last you'll hear from me."

"Thank you, Ms—I mean—Dr. Dumont. We would really like to make this up—"

I hung up, grabbed my stuff, and walked out the door. I had to see this for myself.

Chapter 4

- Ellie

Chad from the hotel wasn't wrong. There sat my car, looking as though I'd been the one who screeched into the ER parking lot and pulled crookedly into the space, not some unknown man who had an emergency of his own. I must've been exhausted because instead of being incredibly pissed off about my stolen car, I wondered what emergency had brought him here. The baby I'd delivered last night was the best reason to end up in ER—seldom were the other reasons so uplifting.

I shook my head to clear it of such thoughts—the car thief didn't need my sympathy—and I pulled open my car door to climb in and head home.

On the seat was a note from a notepad with the Merit Memorial Hospital letterhead. I knew that paper well. The hospital—and my car—had the notepads everywhere.

To Whom It May Concern:
I apologize for taking your car.
I needed to get to the hospital
and I didn't think, I just acted.
Please let me make it up to you.

Again, I apologize.
I can be reached at 555-363-1790
J

Wow. The guy left a note. With a name and number. Well, kind of a name. *J.* When the hotel didn't give me any information on the man who called, I was sure I would never find out who it was.

Wait a minute. Could it be...*James?* Goodness knows he rushed out of the hotel in a hurry last night, and—. What was I thinking? If it was that jerk, James, that was one number I was never going to call.

And frankly, by now I didn't even really care. I got my car back just by walking out of the hospital. That was as good a way as any to wrap up this portion of the whole charity ball debacle I hoped to quickly forget. I had a blissful 36 hours off until I needed to be back at the hospital, and I wasn't going to waste another minute thinking about this.

I tossed the notepad onto my passenger seat and headed for home.

My time off raced by, and I was back in my office at the hospital. The day was going smoothly. No drinks tossed on me, no stolen car when I left my apartment—things were setting up to be a banner day. I'd just turned the corner toward the nurse's station when Jasmine rushed up the hall. As the Nurse Manager for Labor and Delivery, rushing was the only mode she knew.

"Ellie. I've been dying to find you." She reached for my arm, pulled me to the side, and looked around. "Oh, shoot. Never a good idea to say dying in a hospital. Anyhoo—things in the world of birthing have been crazy today—I couldn't find a minute. Hurry! I've only got ten. What happened to you Saturday night?"

I shook my head. "You are not even going to believe. When I left the party, my freaking car had been stolen."

"What? What do you mean stolen? From the hotel?"

"Yes. It was crazy. I rushed out, got to the valet, and my keys were gone. And so was my car. Thank goodness the hotel is so close to the hospital, or I don't know what I would've done."

Jasmine interjected. "You know you could've called me. I hadn't even started drinking yet. My two drinks were spilled all over your dress."

I waved off her belated offer. "I got to the hospital fine on my own. I just high-tailed it to the ER, and then—" I paused for dramatic effect.

"What? You already had drinks spilled on you, and then a stolen car, but you said the delivery went fine. What else could possibly happen?" Jasmine's eyes were wide in question. "No wonder you didn't want to text this saga."

I raised my eyebrows. "You know that guy that spilled our drinks on us?"

Jas gave me a wary look. "Yessss..." she said, dragging out the s.

"He was the baby daddy in the emergency delivery."

Jasmine's eyebrows shot up. "What? No!"

"And he was so caught up in the love fest of his baby's birth, I am pretty positive he didn't even recognize me as the woman he tossed drinks all over."

By this point, Jasmine was shaking her head. "That. Is. Madness."

Her expression quickly changed from disbelief to a little bit disappointed.

"You know, El, for a minute there I thought maybe that guy could actually catch your attention. Who knew he'd not only be a rude jerk but to actually be cheating—or doing whatever he was doing—while his baby was about to be born."

I nodded in complete agreement, then Jas exclaimed, "Wait. What happened with your car?"

I filled her in on the rest of my shift and how I found my car unharmed in the hospital parking lot.

"So that's that," I said. "The car is fine—I'm totally letting the whole thing go. I don't need to have a bunch of back and forths with the people at the hotel. But that crazy night is not really over, yet." I ran my hand through my ponytail. "I won the silent auction prize I bid on at the fundraiser."

"Oh, cool," said Jasmine. "That's a bright spot from the night. What did you win?"

"Another thing you're not going to believe. I won a cooking class at SoBo downtown. It must've been the reference to The Beatles that pulled me in."

But it was more than the Beatles. I knew what it was like to be without food. I'd been hungry so often growing up—my little sister too. It was time I learned how to cook for myself beyond the bare necessities of ramen, PB&J, and takeout.

I continued. "It was being pitched as a way to meet singles. Which you know is ridiculous. Like I have time for that with work and applying for the Tate Award. It's called *The Sgt. Pepper's Lonely Hearts Club Cooking Class.* What the heck was I thinking?"

Jasmine threw her head back and laughed out loud.

"Ellie, the thought of you in a cooking class for singles just made my whole day." She wiped at her eyes, barely able to hold back tears of laughter.

I narrowed my eyes. "You know it's for a good cause. It's to feed kids in need in the city. Even if I don't go, it'll have been worth it."

"Oh, you're gonna go. I'm going to make you go, just so I can hear the stories."

Still laughing, Jasmine began walking away. "I gotta go. Thanks for catching me up. I know you're taking off at the end of the week to work on the Tate, but let's try to do lunch one day if our schedules match up."

She tossed a wave over her shoulder and walked right past Dr. Marks. *Great. Just what I needed. Dr. Marks.* Jasmine shot him a look, which he returned, the jerk.

I grabbed some files from the nurse's station.

"Dumont."

"Marks."

"What happened to you Saturday night?" He asked. "You missed an opportunity to hobnob with the big guys. You know you'll need that more than anyone if you think you're going to win the Tate Award."

Man, he couldn't stand how successful I was. The fact that I had started med school late, and still managed to be one of the youngest doctors with a leadership role in the department drove him crazy.

I smirked. "I'm not worried, Marks—my work stands on its own. I don't need to do all the schmoozing you like to do. I'll take care of my success without having other people step in to help me."

"That's one way to see it. Not sure the award selection committee will see it that way."

I gave my head a small shake. My success ate at him, but the fact that he, of all people, was my greatest competitor ate at me.

He pointed up in the air. "Hey Dumont, you're being paged. Better get that."

The page repeated.

I grabbed a phone at the nurse's station and hit #3. I wondered what might be going on, which snapped me right into putting-out-the-fire emergency mode,

"This is Dr. Dumont."

"Dr. Eleanor Dumont?"

So this wasn't a call from within the hospital.

"Speaking." Who was paging me at the hospital in the middle of a workday?

"Dr. Dumont, this is Officer Paul Kirkpatrick. I'm with the Merit City Police. I'm sorry for the interruption, but you are the sister to Vanessa Ann Dumont, correct?"

Vanessa? I hadn't heard about or from Vanessa in years. We'd been separated since... grade school? And we hadn't spoken since I fought my way into med school. I got a heavy feeling in my stomach. In my life, calls from the cops seldom ended well.

"Yes, I am. What's this about? How did you find me?"

"I'm sorry to have to tell you this, but Vanessa has passed away. You were listed as her next of kin."

Oh, no. My stomach fell right to the floor. But I wouldn't let him know that. I'd hold it together. That's what I did.

"Oh. Um, that's... shocking. She is ... was... younger than me. How did she die?"

"It appears to have been an accidental overdose."

"Oh. Okay." I guess it wasn't a complete surprise. Her drug use was the main reason for our falling out. We watched our mother ruin her own life and ours with drugs. It was bad enough that our mother basically threw her children away. I wasn't going to watch my own sister throw her life away too.

I didn't grapple with my messed-up childhood every day, but it was always there. No one in my adult life knew much about my past, and I wanted to keep it that way. I'd done fine on my own—I was a doctor after all—and I didn't need any pity.

"Well thank you for calling Officer Kirkpatrick. I need to—"

"There's more."

Oh. Right. I'd seen situations like this plenty of times in my work. Someone would need to pay for her burial.

"Of course. You need someone to take care of her burial."

"Dr. Dumont, it's not just her burial. You weren't just listed as Vanessa's next of kin."

"I wasn't? What else is there?"

I heard Office Kirkpatrick inhale deeply.

"You've been named the guardian of her child."

Chapter 5

- Ellie

The guardian. The guardian? Did he say...

"I'm sorry, what did you say?"

"You've been listed as the guardian to her seven-year-old daughter, Dr. Dumont. Her daughter EB. I mean, Emily Beth. She goes by EB."

My stomach had bounced off the floor and was trying to lodge itself in my throat. E and B. Those were my initials, and that was my middle name. Eleanor Beth Dumont. Emily Beth... Dumont? The officer hadn't said differently. After everything my sister and I went through, she basically named her daughter after me, giving her daughter the same middle name and initials as mine? I had to get ahold of myself.

"That's ridiculous. That's crazy. I didn't even know my sister had a daughter. I can't be her guardian."

"I understand this might be—"

"You don't understand anything." Shock. I was in shock. There was no other way to describe it. Vanessa...was dead. And she had left her child to me? Why? What had she been thinking? I hadn't seen her in years, and the last time we spoke had been so contentious I'd resigned myself to never speaking to or seeing her again. And she left me her child?

"I can't take care of a child. I don't even want children." A nurse walked by and gave me a funny look. I lowered my voice. "You're going to have to find someone else."

There was another loud inhale from the other side of the line.

"Okay. This is taking you by complete surprise, I can see that," he said. "Why don't you take a little time, and then Child Protective Services will call you. I'll—"

The Code Blue alert sounded. It drowned out the rest of what the officer was saying with an announcement to report to room 113.

"I have to go," I said.

"Wait, let me—"

I wasn't waiting for anything. Not to be a guardian, and not to hear anything else he had to say.

I hung up and ran to room 113.

My eyelids drooped and I needed to get to bed, but instead, I watched the shopping networks, flipping between the kitchen supplies sale and the home comfort sale. I was taking a cooking class in a couple of days, so eventually, I'd need some supplies. And when I looked around my room, it was abundantly clear my home could use some comfort. My condo itself was beautiful, but it was... minimalist in its furnishings if you were trying to find a polite way to say it.

To be honest, I wasn't there that often. Usually, I was at the hospital. And with all of the foster homes I'd been in and out of, I only had a few objectives when I finally had enough money to get my own place.

    1. It had to be nice. Nothing old or in need of repair—no fixer-uppers. I'd seen enough of those.

2. It had to have a nice bed. Like really nice. I probably shocked the salesman when I bought the top-of-the-line mattress, but I'd had enough of crappy sleeping arrangements.

3. It had to have great bedding. 100% cotton only, and with down comforters.

4. It had to be mine. All mine.

Typically, those things gave me plenty of comfort. Which meant the rest of the place didn't have much. No plush throws over the sofa like they were selling on TV. No knick-knacks. Not a single framed picture of my.... what? My past? The overabundance of friends I had? My... estranged sister? Her child? *How old did that cop say she was...?*

After the bomb that was dropped on me today, it wasn't just my home that could use some comfort. I looked around the room, thinking I might find the answer there. When I didn't, I did what I always did—I glanced at my work email, checked over my progress toward the Tate Award, and went to bed.

I slept like a baby.

Jasmine caught me in my office between scheduled appointments. I'd managed to get my fertility practice associated with the hospital, and I considered myself lucky to be based on the Labor and Delivery floor. I felt like it kept me connected. Plus, it allowed me to take on-call shifts, which I loved.

"Got a second?" Jas asked. "We've got an expectant mother on 2. We could use your input."

"Sure thing." I grabbed my water bottle and joined her in the hall. "What's the situation?"

"She's young," Jasmine said. "Just 19. She's been clean since she found out she's pregnant, but Dr. Jones is doing rounds today, and he didn't like the baby's heartbeat and wanted a second opinion. I said I'd grab you if you were available."

I studied the chart Jasmine handed me and was glad Dr. Jones asked for another look. An elevated heart rate could mean the mother was using again.

"She said she hasn't had a hit in months."

I scoffed. "Yeah, my sister always said that too."

Jasmine pulled her eyebrows together. "What? Your sister? I didn't know you had a sister."

Shoot. Why did I say that? I never referred to Vanessa.

Jasmine seemed a little hurt like I was keeping secrets from her. I guess I was in a way.

"We were estranged. I literally haven't seen or spoken to her in years."

"Still. You and I have known each other for a long time. You would think that something would've come up in reference to her."

Jasmine was my best friend and she knew it. More like—she was my only friend. I was courteous enough to people as was needed, but that didn't make them my friends. Once a week I would bring in donuts to keep my co-workers happy—and distant. Which is where I liked them.

It was totally different with Jasmine. Everyone became her friend—even me. But I saw by her comment she was a bit put out, and I didn't like that. That's the only reason I could think of that compelled me to say what I said next.

We were almost to the patient's room when I said, "Well, something did come up in reference to her. I got a call from a cop yesterday. She died."

Jasmine grabbed my arm and pulled me to a stop. "What? Your sister died yesterday and you didn't tell me? Are you okay? What are you even doing here today?"

Concern and sympathy were written all over her face.

"Jasmine. It's okay. I told you we were estranged. Now let's see this patient."

Her mouth was thinned in concern. "Ok, El. But we're talking about this later."

Not if I could help it.

"Fine, can we go in now? I have another patient I'll need to see soon."

Jasmine gave me another look, and we entered the room.

"We need to talk."

I sighed and leaned back in my chair. The day had flown by, and it was clear Jasmine was not going to let even one extra minute pass without finding out more about my sister.

"Okay. What do you want to know?"

"What do I... what do I... all of it! I want to know all of it. Why have I never heard of her? Why were you estranged? What happened to her? What's her name? But most importantly, are you okay?"

"Yeah, yeah, I am. Thank you for caring, I really appreciate it." I gave her a smile.

"Well, I'm glad you're doing okay. So what happened?"

"Her name is ... was... Vanessa. She overdosed. They think it was accidental, though I am not sure that matters. She had been a drug user all her life. It's why we fell out. I couldn't watch her throw her life away. I had seen enough of that with my mom."

Jasmine twisted her lips with sympathy. She was one of the few people in my life that knew about my mother and a little bit of my childhood in foster care. She didn't know many details about it, but she knew it had happened. She also knew I fought my way out and had basically never looked back. As this conversation proved.

"Oh Ellie, I am sorry. I know it had to be hard for you to watch your mother go through that."

It was hard to watch my mother go through it, but it was even harder on my sister and me, and what we had to go through. As children. Children that she basically gave up on.

"And now your sister too. Poor thing. Poor girl."

Poor girl. Poor girl. Vanessa had a child. A little girl. That was the true poor girl in this story.

"Wait," Jasmine said. "What is that look on your face? I mean, besides the death of a family member and all."

Would I tell her? No. Why would I tell her? I didn't even know this child existed until yesterday. There was no reason to talk about it.

"It's nothing. Really, Jasmine. I just need to pay for the burial and put this behind me. I still have so much to research to complete my application for the Tate, and then there's that stupid cooking class on Thursday, Friday, and Saturday night. Which I'm probably not even—"

"Don't finish that sentence. You work enough as it is, and now you have the death of your sister on top of that. Go to the class. It'll take your mind off all of this, even if just for a little while. And don't forget—I've had your ramen. You need this class."

"You're right, Jas, you're right. I'll go."

"Good. 'Cause really—who messes up ramen?"

She shot me a grin. "You're sure you're okay?"

I nodded. "Yep."

"Okay," she said and left me to my research.

I had one more day left at work this week before I took off Thursday and Friday to dedicate some time to the Tate application and project. The Tate Award was the most prestigious award the hospital gave out. Every year an employee was recognized for their contribution to the advancement of medicine. But the application also took into account things like care for the community and the betterment of society. I wanted to pull some things together from my office before I headed out, and gather some ideas.

I'd like to think that my fertility research into egg maturity in patients with polycystic ovary syndrome and its connection to insulin would make me a shoo-in for the award, but I'd be lying to myself—which I tried hard not to do. I lacked a smidge—okay, more than a smidge—in the care for the community and the betterment of society part of the application. Dr. Marks wasn't wrong when he said the judge's committee might not easily see me as the outright winner.

But, come on. I was a doctor. Every minute of my work was for the good of the community and the betterment of society. Of course, every doctor could say that. Hence, the requirement for the Tate—something that would differentiate me from the others.

I sighed and threw down my pen, struggling to come up with a single idea that would make me stand out from my peers. I thought of my sister, and of her child. Her daughter whom I knew nothing about. Guardian. She named me as guardian...

Tension crawled up my back and rounded over my shoulders.

My Tate research wasn't going anywhere...maybe I should research something else.

I took a deep breath and logged onto the internet.

Chapter 6

- Ellie

My mind was all over the place as I walked into SoBo Restaurant—short for South Bound—for my cooking class. I did an internet search last night, then this morning I called Child Protective Services, and the conversation had my head spinning. When I signed up for this cooking class, I was thinking about learning to cook for myself. Was I really suddenly considering cooking for a child?

The restaurant was gorgeous, with a fabulous mix of vintage and modern—scraped brick on the walls, acid-etched concrete floors, sparkling crystal chandeliers, and sheet metal table tops. I knew my life was super busy, but how had I never been here?

In a room to the back of the restaurant, there were six tables set up, each with cooking workstations, and people were already paired up. All but one. I walked up to the table and took a second to admire the man who had his back towards me. He looked good from behind. He was taller than me, which was a plus. And I liked the back of his head, as crazy as that was. His super short haircut from the back showed off the beautiful shape of his skull. What? We studied a lot of skulls in med school. I liked them. So sue me.

He talked animatedly with the couple at the table behind him, as though he had known them for years. Maybe he had. Maybe all of these people were here as couples, and not using the event to meet someone, even though it was billed as a singles event.

I reached the table and started to say hello, when he turned around, and *oh, nooooo!*

It was James. James of the lovers' quarrel at the charity ball, James of the spilled drinks, James of the baby daddy *James.*

I spun on my heel and quickly walked towards the exit when I heard him rush up behind me.

"Hey. Hey! Wait up. Where are you going?" I heard him say.

I didn't slow down in the slightest and made my way out to the sidewalk, where I headed to the parking garage. What I didn't need tonight—was James.

"Hey, we haven't even met. Where are you—"

I whirled around, unable to keep my thoughts to myself. For a minute there I thought I would get away without an actual conversation, but it appeared that he really wanted to have one. Okay—talk it is then.

"Oh, we may not have met," I said. "But I wouldn't expect someone like you to remember me, anyway. Not with all the other women you're already juggling."

"All the other women? What are you talking about?" He had the audacity to actually give me a look of innocence. He probably practiced that exact expression in the mirror.

"Oh my gosh. I have to spell it out for you? The hospital charity ball? Last Saturday at the Luxor?"

"Look, I don't know you—"

"As I've already established," I said. "And I don't want to know you. So just let me get my car."

"Wait, wait. I don't know what's going on."

I threw my hands up. "I saw you. Last weekend. With your girlfriend at the charity ball. You were having some kind of argument and were pretty hard to miss. You were especially hard to miss because when you ran out, you spilled drinks—all over me!"

The color drained from James's face. Yeah, I thought so.

"That was you? I'm so sorry, it was an emergency, I had to—"

I scoffed. "I don't want your apologies. And guess what? I know it was an emergency. Wanna know how I know?"

"How... do you... know?" he asked slowly.

"Because 30 minutes later I saw you with another woman. A different woman. Not your girlfriend. I saw you again. At the hospital. Where I. Delivered. Your baby."

"Oh no. Okay. Just a minute, you're right, you're right I was at both—"

"I know I'm right, and I don't need to hear anything else from someone like you. My gosh, you bring a baby into this world, and then five days later you're at a singles event, trying to pick up someone new? What is wrong with you? Never mind, I know what's wrong with you, I've seen it a million times, I've—"

"You're wrong. You're wrong about everything."

That didn't sound right.

"Wait." I paused. "Just a second ago you said I was right."

"You're right that I was at both places," he said. "Completely wrong about everything else."

"Now what are *you* talking about?"

"First, that woman at the charity ball was not my girlfriend. We're each other's dates when we need one. That's it. But more importantly, that baby is not mine."

I raised my eyebrows. "And you expect me to believe that?"

"Yeah, I do. Though I don't know why I care, after the way you just yelled at me. That baby is my sister's. I'm the Uncle. Uncle James."

I took a slight step back and gave my head a gentle shake. "Oh." Okay. So I'm shocked. Just a little. "Well, how is he?"

"Who, the baby? He's great."

"And your sister?"

"She's good, too."

"Good, good," I said.

It was obvious by the frown on his face he was not thrilled with me at the moment.

"You know, I thought...the baby," I stuttered. "You were there...she named him after you...what..."

He cocked an eyebrow.

Wow. Did I get that wrong. It took a lot for me to be embarrassed; my rough childhood basically cured me of that. But I felt heat rising to my cheeks over my big blunder. I bit my lip, and looked around the sidewalk, anywhere but at him. At James.

James reached out and gently touched my arm.

"Hey," he said. "We've really gotten off to a bad start here. Let's start over. First—I'm James. I'm sorry I spilled drinks all over you." He gave me a lopsided smile.

"Um, Dr. Dumont. Dr. Eleanor. And I'm so sorry I assumed."

"Careful about making assumptions. They can make an as—"

"I know," I said. "I do. I'm sorry."

He gave me a small smile.

"Well, Dr. Eleanor, how about it?" He pointed at the restaurant. "Are we going to go in there and learn how to cook, or what?"

"Welcome to *Sgt. Pepper's Lonely Hearts Club Cooking Class*." Chef Mike was a big man, and by that I mean huge. Like if you saw him on the street you would be confident he was a linebacker in the NFL. But nope, here he was, chef hat and all, gearing us up for a night of cooking.

"If you haven't already done so, take a second to introduce yourself to your partner. This is a singles event, so you'll meet everyone here before our three days are up, but you'll spend most of your time with the person you are with now. My wife and I fell in love over food, while The Beatles played in the background, so I know it can happen. By the time the classes are over, our goal is to be *Sgt. Pepper's* No Longer Lonely *Hearts Club Cooking Class*."

Someone let out a wolf whistle, while the rest of the class cheered and applauded. I clapped politely—I was a bit more reserved than the rest of this class it seemed. I was here for the food, not the whole singles thing. The Beatles' *Sgt. Pepper's* album began to play—Chef Mike was definitely a fan. Being a Beatles fan myself, I thought this class might turn around, compared to how it started.

Chef Mike clapped his hands to pull our attention.

"First, I want to thank you all for being here tonight. Everything we're using for the class has been donated, so 50% of the money we collected from the silent auction goes to the new children's wing at the hospital and 50% will go to children who are hungry right here in Merit. This will make a huge difference in their lives, so thank you."

My stomach did a little dip like it always did when I thought about hungry children and what my sister and I went through. And more importantly, what kids were going through today. It was the biggest reason I bid on this event.

I mentally shook myself out of that thought. Vanessa and her daughter were bringing up a lot of my past, and I was so not interested.

Chef Mike continued to go over how the classes would be conducted.

"Our *Lonely Hearts Club Cooking Class* is going to kick off the night with "Food that Puts You in the Mood.""

The classroom broke into chuckles, and someone called out, "I don't need food to get in the mood," and a lot of laughter followed.

Chef Mike laughed along. "You might not need food, but when it comes to love and love stories, there's a reason so many movies and books feature food. For one thing, it engages all of your senses. Let's start with the most obvious—your sight. Come on, everyone, gather around this table."

We moved en masse towards the table, where Chef Mike had an array of food items.

"Go on, pick them up. You might be surprised how many of these items can turn our thoughts into monkey brain, and the next thing you know you've got more than food on the mind."

He picked up a smooth, large, deep aubergine eggplant, which again got a big laugh from the group.

"The eggplant has never been elevated to such heights of popularity as it has with the advent of texting."

A tall blonde man—his name tag said Brett—reached for the eggplant, and stroked it lovingly. "This seems about right," he said. He grinned at the group and effectively established himself as the class clown.

"Alright, everyone, grab something from the platter, head back to your stations and we'll move into our "Setting the Mood with Food" section."

"Who knew this class would be so filled with innuendo," James said. He reached for a very full, very ripe, orangey-red peach. I just shook my head.

There was a lot of laughter and good-natured ribbing from the group as we selected items from the platter. Choices included bright yellow bananas, big fluffy muffins, a trio of tiny little tacos in taco stands, long and thick cucumbers, the peaches and eggplants, a bunch of asparagus, and a mystery box with a red X on it that no one reached for. I was tempted—I was very tempted. I went with a richly hued banana, instead.

Back at our table, Chef Mike asked us to meet the people around us.

James turned to the table at our back, and extended his hand to Brett, the class clown.

"I'm James, nice to officially meet you." he said, shaking Brett's hand, "And this is Eleanor. I mean, Dr. Eleanor."

"Nice to meet you, James, and Dr. Eleanor. What kind of doctor are you?" Brett shook hands with James, then extended his hand to me.

"Baby Doc. I deliver babies."

"Oh, so you like kids?"

I laughed, really for the first time all evening. "You could say that. But I especially like kids that belong to other people." I had no intention of being a parent. I didn't exactly have a role model on how to be a good mother, other than exactly how *not* to be a good mother.

Brett laughed. "I hear that. You can always spoil them and then walk away. I have two nieces, and the leaving is as good as the coming." He tilted his head down, looked up through his eyelashes, and said, "Do you know what I'm talking about?"

Oh my gosh, this guy. I *was* in a class for singles, so I gave a little chuckle. Brett laughed a little harder, then turned to his partner.

"James and Eleanor, this is my lovely partner—who I am happy to have met here tonight—Shauna."

We shook hands with a pretty brunette, petite and curvy in all the right places, with a beautiful smile that lit up her face. "Nice to meet you guys," she said. "Here's hoping that we find what we were looking for when we signed up for this class."

"Agreed," I said. I thought about expanding my cooking repertoire and then about maybe cooking for Vanessa's daughter, EB.

Brett still held onto his eggplant, and he motioned over to the two figs sitting on Shauna's side of the cooktop.

"I'm not sure how those figs are supposed to inspire amorous feelings," he said. "They are so small they remind me of middle school and 'The Itty Bitty Titty Committee.'"

Without missing a beat, Shauna fired right back. "Oh, I'm sure you're wishing for something that would need 'over-the-shoulder-boulder-holders,' but you're thinking of the wrong sex." Shauna picked up the two figs and rolled them around in one hand. "These little guys need protection. Like an 'under-the-butt-nut-hut.'"

Brett looked stunned. Stunned and speechless. Then he burst out laughing. "You are feisty. Where did you learn that?"

By this point, even I was laughing, and Shauna gave a coy little smile and shrugged her shoulders. "Brothers. Four of 'em."

James's eyebrows shot up in surprise. "That's just like my family. Four boys and a girl."

We were interrupted when Chef Mike got our attention by grabbing up the box with the red X. "Okay, before we get into tonight's dishes, there are two more things I want to share with you. Our last day of class is going to be a little competition. We're going to do some taste testing from each team, and vote on the best taste and the best presentation. So keep that in mind as we go along."

The class buzzed a bit as we took in this information. James gave me a little elbow in the side and arched an eyebrow.

"I'm actually a pretty good cook," he said. "Maybe we can take this competition."

I loved a good challenge, and apparently so did James. I preferred to do things on my own, though, so hopefully, James and I could divide up duties. I didn't really cook, but surely after three days of lessons, I'd be able to pull off something.

"That sounds good. I can't cook at all, but I love to win."

"Okay, everyone, last but not least—the mystery box." Chef Mike held up the box. "I'm surprised nobody picked it up. Usually, someone can't bear to resist it, sitting right there in the middle of all of the mood-food unmentionables. But this box most definitely needs to be mentioned. I know we've been joking around a lot tonight, but relationships, especially relationships that lead to intimacy, are no laughing matter." Chef Mike dropped the box down onto the cooktop. "You really need to take care of each other, 'cause if you don't, things are going to get... spoiled." He gave us a big grin. "See what I did there? Spoiled? Like—food spoils?" He chuckled to himself, then opened up the box.

"If you don't take care of yourself and your partner, it could lead to a lot of unwanted things in your life. Possibly even..." Chef Mike dumped the box out in front of him. "A wicked case of the crabs." And out spilled cans and cans of crab meat.

"Eww, gross," Shauna said behind us, while Brett laughed and James shook his head. Two tables over, one of the guys muttered, "Too bad you can't get rid of crabs as easy as Chef Mike is going to get rid of those cans."

James motioned toward the guy who made the comment. "I know you deliver babies, but it sounds like that guy might need a doctor."

I mimicked Shauna with my own, "Eww, gross. I'll stick to the babies, thanks."

James chuckled at that.

The cans of crab got passed around the room, and Chef Mike's assistants dropped off boxes of ingredients to each station.

"When I say aphrodisiac, what food immediately comes to mind?" asked Chef Mike.

A couple at the front of the room both shouted out "oysters!" then turned to each other and said "jinx."

"Oysters. Exactly. The word aphrodisiac comes from the Greek goddess Aphrodite, goddess of love and beauty. And if you've seen any paintings of Aphrodite, she is often seen coming out of a clamshell. So seafood and shell foods are considered aphrodisiacs. Things like lobster, crab, and oysters. Remember I mentioned food and all of the senses. What happens when you are eating those shellfish? There is a lot of slurping and swallowing, and licking of the fingers—and a lot of people consider that a turn-on."

I glanced around the room and saw mostly amused faces. All of this talk about intimacy and turn-ons, and we hadn't even cooked anything yet.

And now I was thinking about James.

Oh great, now I was really thinking about James.

James dove into our box of supplies and pulled out all of the ingredients and recipe cards. He grouped things together, like items with like items. Spices, cheeses, and chocolates. Mmm, chocolate. Finally, we were getting somewhere.

"Tonight we're going to cover a few things, get you used to some of the basics so that tomorrow we can dive right in," Chef Mike said. "We're "Setting the Mood with Food." So we'll start with a little appetizer I call Kickin' Crab Dip, a warm spicy crab and artichoke dip, with a crust of melted parmesan and mozzarella cheese. Crab, spicy foods, and even artichokes are considered aphrodisiacs. They supposedly open up those blood vessels and get the blood pumping. We're going to go over this recipe step by step, and you guys are going to follow along. Remember my motto for all you newbies who have never really cooked before, but especially for all of you here tonight, at a singles event. When you really like someone, and you've made the decision to cook for them, just remember, 'If you can't be interesting, at least your food can be!'"

Even I laughed out loud at that one. Chef Mike was highly entertaining.

James gave me a wide smile, and I returned it.

"Are you ready Dr. Eleanor? Let's do this."

Chapter 7

- *Ellie*

I was struggling with James's hands. I don't mean literally struggling with them—we weren't having a tug of war or anything—but I was oddly fascinated. Almost as fascinated as I had originally been with the shape of his head. My gosh, how long had it been since I'd been on a date? This was getting ridiculous.

He was grating the parmesan cheese for the crab and artichoke dip, and I found myself just staring. And then he found me just staring.

"What?" he said, trying not to laugh.

"Um, what do you do?" I blurted out.

"What? I'm grating cheese."

"No. No, I know that, what do you do for a living?" I asked.

"Oh. I'm a builder. Cross Construction. Ever heard of it?"

"Can't say that I have. I'm not really up on the building trade." But that did explain those rough-looking, scarred, large calloused hands. So different from the doctors' hands I saw at the hospital all day. So different from mine. Mine were capable, yes. But soft. Nothing like his.

"Yeah, understandable. If you haven't built a home in the past five years, or if you don't live where there's building going on, there's not a lot of reason to know me. My business is actually why I was at the hospital charity event last week."

He handed me the measuring cups. "According to the recipe we need ¾ cup of Parmesan cheese placed in a medium-sized mixing bowl, with an additional ¼ cup to set aside."

I grabbed the mixing bowls and measured out what we needed. "Why would your business bring you there? Were you a sponsor?"

"No, not yet. The ticket price for just attending is pretty steep, and I'm not quite big enough to pay for sponsorship. But that's one of my goals. I was there for two reasons. I'm sure you know it's a great cause—all of the ticket sales go to the new children's wing for the hospital. And I was also there to meet anyone I could who actually works at the hospital."

I raised an eyebrow. "I work at the hospital, so that's a start. Why do you want to know people who work there?"

"The new children's wing. It's time for my business to move into doing commercial building, and I love the thought of building the new children's wing. Meeting people who work at the hospital might open some doors for me."

By this time, James had me blending cream cheese, sour cream, red pepper flakes, and parmesan together, while he quartered the canned artichoke hearts.

"Oh, that looks good," he said. "See how smooth and creamy it is? You're doing great."

I laughed out loud.

"What's funny? You really are doing great."

"The longer we are in this class, the easier it is to hear everything as a double entendre." I mustered up a breathy voice. 'Ooohhh it's so smooth and creamy. Ellie, you're doing so good.'"

James's eyes went wide. Then he smiled a little smile, leaned in close to me, and dropped his voice. "Maybe I'm following Chef Mike's suggestion, and just setting the mood." He lifted his cutting board and poured the chopped artichokes in the bowl. Our hands brushed as he took over the stirring, and I giggled and looked away.

I giggled! What was happening to me?

With the small smile still on his face, he continued to stir, giving me a little side-eye as he did. And now I was embarrassed. I could feel the heat rising up the back of my neck. Why did I giggle?

"You called yourself Ellie," James said.

"What?"

"Just now. When you were all...you know. You said 'Ellie, you're doing so good.'"

"Oh. Right. Ellie. My friends call me Ellie." Not that there were a ton of those around.

James turned fully towards me. "Can I call you Ellie?"

I don't know what the look on my face must've said, but James was quick to re-state his request.

"I mean, can I call you Dr. Ellie?"

I smiled at James. I did like him. He was super friendly, and even kind of charming.

"Sure. Call me Dr. Ellie."

"Dr. Ellie it is."

"Now that we've got all of the Kickin' Crab Dip in the oven, it's time for the 'Is that a Rocket in Your Pocket Salad.'" Chef Mike burst out laughing. "I couldn't help myself. It's not really called that, it just came to me in the moment. Does anyone know what 'rocket' is?"

He was still kind of chuckling to himself when a woman towards the front of the room called out. "Arugula?"

"Yep, that's it—arugula. We're going to put together a light salad to counter the heaviness of the Kickin' Crab Dip. Our salad is going to be mainly arugula with some mixed greens,

candied pecans, strawberries, and a light pomegranate vinaigrette. We're working two aphrodisiacs into this one—strawberries and pomegranate. And of course, if you want to be a
bit on the crass side, you can call it 'Rocket in Your Pocket'
salad. I know I will. Okay, let's get started with the pecans."
Chef Mike was still laughing at his own joke.

James took the lead again, and I was surprised at how easily
I let him. I tended to take control of situations. It was one of
the many reasons I liked being a doctor so much. Yes, people
definitely had to help you out, but I called the shots, and
controlled what was going on. That's the way I preferred it.
But James was the better cook, so I was okay. For now.

"Why were you at the charity ball?" James asked. "Were
you required to go because you work there? And again—sorry
about those drinks." James measured out sugar for the pecan
glaze, then handed me a little carton of eggs.

"Wait. What am I doing with these eggs?"

James laughed. "Relax, Dr. Ellie. We're just going to separate
them. Have you really never separated an egg before?"

"Unless we're suddenly talking about a woman's
eggs—which I am pretty sure we're not —then no. I haven't."

James bit his bottom lip and tried not to laugh when Brett
chimed in from behind us. "Hey, did you just call Dr. Eleanor,
Dr. Ellie? Can I call you Dr. Ellie? Eleanor is so formal."

Brett raised his eyebrows at me expectantly, and so did
Shauna.

"I love the name Ellie," she said. "It's such a pretty name. It
goes with how pretty you are. And it's fun too."

Fun. Huh. I doubted I'd ever been referred to as fun, though
I guess Shauna wasn't really calling me fun, just my name. I
looked at these three virtual strangers, all smiling and seemingly so open. Why were they so open? We barely knew each
other. I didn't get it, but the whole atmosphere here had been
warm and welcoming, so what the heck.

I smiled at the three of them. "Yes. Please, call me Dr. Ellie"

"So why were you at the charity ball?" James circled around to his earlier question, though I'd rather hoped he wouldn't. We had finished eating the Kickin' Crab Dip, which was delicious, and then cleansed our palate, as Chef Mike had said, with the Pocket Rocket Salad.

I had no idea making a vinaigrette would be so easy, and so easy to change up for a completely new taste. Just using different kinds of vinegar, like red wine, balsamic, or pomegranate like we used tonight. Or adding things like French, Dijon, or stone-ground mustard. Chef Mike had lots of samples for us to try, with varying ingredients.

I liked how it felt like chemistry class, which I was very familiar with. We moved on to our last recipe of the night, Molten Lava Cake. Chef Mike had way too much fun talking about chocolate, and all of the ways it could be used. Several people shouted out ideas on how to use it, which definitely had to do with eating, but had nothing to do with cooking.

I was dodging James's question. I could take the easy way out and go with what he guessed—that I was required to be there. But that felt a little deceptive, especially since he had been so quick to share throughout the evening.

"I wasn't really required to be there," I said. "I was there because my mentor suggested it would help with my application for an award that the hospital gives. The Tate Award."

James got a bright look in his eye. "You did say you like to win. What's the award about?"

He continued to butter and flour the small dishes that the individual cakes would be baked in. I wasn't sure why they had to be buttered and floured twice, but I was listening to Chef Mike.

"When it comes to baking," he said, "the rules are there for a reason. Follow them. Later, when you have gained some confidence and made some mistakes of your own, you can bend the rules. But just a little. Baking is much more scientific than cooking, and there's not a lot of wiggle room. You can get away with a lot more in cooking."

Maybe I would actually like to bake. Again, science.

I was melting semi-sweet chocolate chips in a double-boiler on the cooktop. Double-boiler. I was learning a whole new lingo.

"It's an award for the advancement of medicine," I said. "But it also has a whole element around community service and the betterment of society, and my mentor thought mingling a bit with my co-workers might shed some light on how I could beef up that part of my application." I didn't mention that 'mingling' wasn't exactly my strong suit. It always felt like such a waste of time.

"My building business does community service all the time. It's not that hard to do."

My reaction was instantaneous. "Ha. I'm having a hard enough time right now with the thought of community service, and it's for my own sister."

James looked at me with confusion. "What do you mean?"

Oh, shoot. I did not want to get into this. Especially not with James. I hadn't even told Jasmine about my sister's daughter. And this whole fun, flirty night with James would be dashed if he knew about my past. If he knew about her.

"Nothing. It's nothing. I've got it covered."

He squinted his eyes a bit like he didn't believe me, but he didn't push.

"We try to build at least three homes a year with Habitat for Humanity," he said. "Would that help your application?"

My mouth dropped open. Just like that? I mean, I knew we were getting to know each other and we got along, but just like that he was opening a door for me to get in some community service?

James laughed and reached over and tipped my chin closed. With that little touch, my breath caught, and my stomach pulled.

"Dr. Ellie," he said. "It's not that big of a deal. Lots of people help. You can help if you want to."

"Ellie," I said with a tremor to my voice that I hoped he couldn't hear. "Just call me Ellie."

And James smiled.

We all stood around the group table and ate our Molten Lava Cake. It. Was. Delicious. I laughed to myself and thought about how Jasmine was rubbing off on me. I was beginning to sound like her, even in my head.

"It's good, right?" James stuck his finger in the fresh whipped cream on the side of his plate and licked it off. Suddenly those earlier comments from the class about everything you could do with chocolate came to mind. You could do those things with whipped cream, too. And I wondered if James and I should do it together.

"Um, right. Right. It is good." I looked around the room and hoped James couldn't read my mind and the dirty thoughts I was having about him, but I bet he knew. He seemed to notice a lot.

"And so easy to make." James took another bite. "And rich. No one would guess how easy it was."

"I don't think everyone would agree with you. Some of these cakes look like complete fails."

He looked around the room and laughed. "You're right. It looks like the couple from the front of the room couldn't get theirs out of the ramekin. And the ones next to us just have a bunch of goo on their plates. Do you think it tastes any good? They don't seem to be eating it."

Shauna, who stood on the other side of James, responded. "It's hard to ruin chocolate, but maybe they succeeded. They just keep pushing it around. Oh, wait. She took a bite of the whipped cream. Maybe they got something right."

Chef Mike clapped his hands. "We have 15 minutes before your first *Lonely Hearts Club Cooking Class* is over, and I want to make sure that everyone learns something about each other. I know a lot of you have met, but we're going to do an icebreaker. I like to do this at the end of the class when everyone is more relaxed and in the spirit of things."

James and I exchanged glances.

"Grab the index card in front of you, and I want you to write down the last meal or thing you prepared for yourself, not including what you made in class tonight. Don't think too hard, just write it down and pass it up to me."

Everyone grabbed a card and began writing. Chef Mike pulled the cards together. "I'm going to say what's on the card, and you guys are going to guess who prepared the meal. The first card—it's a classic. PB&J."

The class laughed and looked around at each other. James immediately said "Dr. Ellie. My partner." I burst out laughing, and more names were shouted out. By the time we had it all figured out, there were three of us in the class who had last made PB&J, and yes, I was one of them.

"When it comes to food and cooking—and I use the term cooking here loosely—everyone has their own personal likes and dislikes. Even with PB&J. What type of bread, crust or crustless, the ratio of peanut butter to jelly. I'm going to share this tip I have. Let's say you're not going to eat your sandwich right away, like you're packing it for lunch or a picnic. You know how sometimes the jelly seeps through the bread, and things get a bit soggier than you want? It's even happened to me, and I'm a renowned chef."

We all laughed as Chef Mike continued. "Next time you're making a PB&J, spread a very thin layer of peanut butter on the piece of bread where you are going to spread the jelly. That thin layer will basically seal the jelly into the sandwich, and keep it from leaking through your bread."

The class broke into applause over Chef Mike's suggestion, and he bowed his head, then shook it from side to side, and laughed. "You know it's bad when it's the PB&J tip that gets the biggest applause of the night." He clapped his hands together. "Looks like my work is cut out for me for the next two days. I need to get you guys cooking."

Chef Mike went through the rest of the cards, with spaghetti being the only other meal that was duplicated by two people. Other meals included a couple of variations on chicken and a couple of frozen meals which really got to Chef Mike. Brett had made hamburgers, Shauna had made grilled chicken, and James was the surprise of the class. He had made a cheese souffle with ham and asparagus. I hadn't even guessed him for that meal, and he was my partner.

He arched an eyebrow and gave me a little smirk. "What? I told you I could cook."

Before I could reply, Chef Mike continued. "Ok, I want all the PB&J's together, the spaghetti's together, the chicken's together, hamburger, you go with spaghetti, and James. You of the 'cheese souffle.' Please, please join the frozen dinners, 'cause they just might make me cry, and they need all the help they can get. Get together, introduce yourselves, and tell each other what was going on in your lives that led to the meal you cooked. Again, I use the term loosely."

We broke into our groups, and I introduced myself to the other two PB&Jers, Kevin and Jamal. They had both met earlier in the night, so I was the newcomer.

"I'll start," said Kevin. "I actually can cook—really. My grandmother is Italian, and I've been cooking with her since I was little. It's surprising I'm not in the spaghetti group, because I make spaghetti with homemade sauce at least once a week. But I'd had a really long day at work, and I just wanted to eat something quick but good while I watched some Sports-Center before I hit the hay. I can't even remember the last time I had a peanut butter and jelly, but I had some homemade bread from my grandma, and it just popped into my mind. It was delicious."

"What do you do that you were so exhausted?" I asked.

Kevin shrugged his shoulders. "Nothing too exciting. I'm a CPA, and one of my clients thinks someone might be embezzling from his company, so I've been combing through the books."

Jamal chimed in. "I don't know, that sounds kind of exciting. Getting into all of the details, seeing what kind of things people do to try to pull a fast one, and you get to be the one who figures it out. Pretty cool."

"What do you do, Jamal?" I asked.

"I'm a teacher. Seventh-grade math. I can definitely appreciate digging into the numbers."

"And why were you making peanut butter and jelly?"

"I tutor kids after school in my classroom. And the kids are always starving. If I think hunger is impacting the tutoring session, I'll pull out the PB&J. Unfortunately I haven't been able to figure out how to keep ice cold milk to go with it, so I just go with water." He shook his head. "It's not the same."

My stomach did that dip thing again when I thought of starving kids. I knew being hungry while I was growing up impacted my studies.

Kevin said, "That's awesome, man. I bet those kids love that." Then he turned to me.

"So you're a doctor." He nodded to my nametag, where I'd written Dr. Eleanor. Usually, I was with other doctors when I had a name tag on, and they almost all started with Dr. In this setting, even though I was very proud of all that I'd achieved by myself, I suddenly realized how pretentious I must sound.

Not what I was going for if I'd thought about it at all. "What was going on in your day that ended up with peanut butter?"

"Similar to you," I said. "Just a super long day at the hospital, and it was the easiest thing. But unlike you, I can barely cook at all. I really needed this class."

"All right, everyone, let's get back to your workstations and wrap up," said Chef Mike. "And then we'll do it all again tomorrow. Great class everyone."

There was a smattering of applause, some whistles, and a lot of talking as we went back to our tables. The first night of cooking class seemed to be a success.

I approached my table and stepped up between Brett and James. Shauna joined us.

"James," she said. "Cheese souffle? I can barely spell souffle, let alone make one. I'm impressed."

"So am I," said Brett. "When this class is over, you can give us a lesson, James." He included Shauna and me in that 'us', which was touching. Who were these people?

"I'd love that. Let's. Dr. Ellie, are you in?" Shauna bounced on her toes a little bit. It appeared as though Shauna and Brett were hitting it off.

"Um, sure. I mean, if I can. Baby Doc and all. My schedule's all over the place. I don't have a lot of free time."

"We'll make it work," James said, then he put his arms around both Shauna and me. "Between this class and some additional lessons from me, you'll be cooks yet." He pulled us in for a little one-armed hug, and let us go.

Both Shauna and I smiled at James's antics.

But deep down, I was really smiling about that one-armed hug.

Now, what would I need to do to get another one?

Chapter 8

- James

I watched Dr. Eleanor—scratch that—Ellie, gather her things, getting ready to leave the cooking class. I found her attractive, and not just her looks. Sometimes she was funny and then she was stiff, and the combination intrigued me. I was surprised I hadn't noticed her at the ball or in the delivery room. And I wasn't ready for the class to be over. I'd been having fun with her. With the class as a whole, in fact. I couldn't remember the last time I'd had such a good time.

"So, Ellie," I said. "You're going to be here tomorrow, right?"

"I plan on it. Getting through the basics today was great, but I really need help on more pedestrian things than chocolate lava cake. I need a good dinner meal or two. So yeah, I'll be here."

"Great. And again, I'm sorry—"

"Forget about it, James. I'll see you tomorrow night."

"See ya."

With a small wave, Ellie left the restaurant. But oddly it was like she was leaving me. I rubbed at the center of my chest, trying to ease the tightness that I felt there.

"Hey James, Shauna and I are going to head over to McGuire's Pub for a beer. Care to join?" Brett asked.

"Sure," I said. "But I'll have to make it quick—early start tomorrow."

We headed out towards McGuire's, a well-known Irish pub. I hadn't been there in a while, but the last time at least three different people over the course of the night had broken out into "Danny Boy," and the whole bar joined in. Got a laugh out of me every time.

Shauna was on the outside of the sidewalk, closest to the road, so I slid up beside her, and moved her to the middle of the sidewalk.

"Such a gentleman," she said, and I gave her a grin.

"Did you know," I said, "that a man walking on the outside of the sidewalk as a courtesy originated during the days of carriages and horses? It meant if mud or something more offensive splashed from the road, it would get on the man, not on the woman."

Shauna gave me a slight nudge on the shoulder. "Well these days being on the inside can still keep mud from splashing on me—and I'm hoping there isn't anything more offensive than that."

"Speaking of offensive—since I'm giving a little history les-son—if you go further back in time, it was the opposite, and it was the *man* who walked on the inside. Want to guess why?"

Brett and Shauna gave each other quizzical looks, and Brett said, "I don't know. There were still horses and carts going by on the road, right?"

"There were," I said with a grin. "But there was something much worse. People opened up their windows and just tossed out the contents of their chamber pots, right onto the street."

"Ew, gross," Shauna said. "That is offensive. Better it hitting you guys than me, that's for sure."

Shauna laughed, and Brett joined her.

"We've gone from aphrodisiacs to chamber pots," Brett said. "I can't wait to see what topic we hit next."

Brett reached for the door to McGuire's and held it open for Shauna and me to walk through. As expected, we were met with a rousing rendition of "Danny Boy." We all joined in, and Shauna headed to a booth towards the back. Brett moved to the bar to order for us and returned with beers all around.

"Cheers to our first successful night of cooking class!" He said.

We brought our glasses together in a hearty toast and I took my first drink.

"So James, do you really want to give us all another cooking lesson when our class is over? Or were you just being nice in the moment?" Shauna twirled a cardboard drink coaster around with her finger.

"No, I want to. I'm a pretty good cook and based on the last meals you guys cooked you both seem like you're okay in the kitchen. But Ellie can't cook at all. So yeah, I'd like to do it."

"Really, Dr. Ellie can't cook? She actually took the class to learn, not to meet someone single?" asked Brett. He gave a little side glance towards Shauna, who sat next to him on the booth bench.

"I don't know about her relationship status. But she gave me the distinct impression that learning to cook was really why she was in the class." I found myself a little disappointed as I stated that out loud.

"What about you?" asked Brett. "Obviously, you know how to cook—so you took the class to meet someone?"

Did I? It had been a while...

But it wasn't anything I wanted to think about right now, so I dodged the question.

"I bought the class as a charity donation."

"What about Dr. Ellie? She seems nice," said Shauna. "And like I said earlier, she's so pretty." Shauna raised her eyebrows at me as she drank her beer.

"Smart and beautiful. Just like Shauna here," Brett said.

Shauna nudged into Brett's shoulder. "Shut up," she said, but she gave a little smile when she said it.

They were right. Dr. Ellie was smart and beautiful, and we'd had a lot of fun together. Or at least we had once the whole "really, I'm not someone's baby daddy" conversation was behind us.

"It was good. I guess I'll just see where it goes." With all the planning and preparation I had to do in my construction business, I tended to let my personal life take its own course. Besides, I was always in a serious relationship, and since I currently wasn't in one, I was committed to building my business. This was not the time to be taking a break. No matter how hot Dr. Ellie was.

I took a drink. "What about you guys?" I motioned between the two of them "Dare I ask?"

At my comment, Shauna's cheeks turned pink, and she shifted around in her seat. She took a big swallow of her beer, and this time it was Brett who leaned into her.

"I definitely took the class to meet someone," said Brett. "I'm so tired of the bar scene, and I would never do a dating app. I didn't think this would be such a success." Brett leaned into Shauna again and looked right at her. "But it was a lot of fun, right?"

Shauna laughed. "It was. I like the cooking tips, but I took the class to meet someone too." She turned to Brett. "I think we're off to a pretty good start."

They held up their glasses for their own personal "cheers," which I took as my cue to wrap up the evening.

I finished my drink and stood to go. "Thanks for including me tonight, but I need to hit the road."

"How early is your day tomorrow?" Brett asked.

"Very. Need to be at the construction site by six. I see as many sites as I can on Fridays, just to keep an eye on things."

"Ok, man, we'll see you tomorrow night in class, right?" Brett stuck out his hand to shake.

"Sure thing," I said

Shauna slid out of the booth and gave me a hug. "See you tomorrow night, James."

"Night guys. See ya." I gave them both a wave as I headed out, happy to have shared a bit more time with them, but I really wished it was Ellie that had hugged me goodnight.

5:15 am rolled around quickly, but I was used to it. I'd done some type of building or construction for most of my life, so early starts were nothing new.

I met up with the foreman of the Zimmer site, my good friend Mario. He was great at his job, which made both the clients and me happy.

"Hey Boss, how you doin' today?" Mario greeted me with a handshake, and I greeted him with a cup of coffee. "You know that's not how it usually works right?" he asked. "The employee is supposed to bring the boss the coffee, not the other way around."

"I know, but who would I be if I did things like everyone else?" I took a quick look around the site. The Zimmer home was only our third foray into the 'modern' style of home building, so I liked to start my Fridays here. It was the build most likely to have problems since it was new to us. I was a classics kind of guy. I loved traditional homes and history, but I'd branched out over the past year and added more modern offerings. I was trying to get into commercial building as well. Hence the hospital fundraiser.

And now I was thinking about Dr. Ellie. Bad enough I thought about her all night, the whole time I was out with Brett and Shauna, and now here I was beginning the day with her on my mind. It was going to be a long day until cooking class.

"That's why I love you, Boss—you're not like other bosses." Mario motioned to the site. "Everything here is on track, going as planned."

"Good. Progress looks good, too. The floor-to-ceiling windows on the second level are better than I expected."

"Yeah, it was a stroke of genius when you suggested the inside trim on the black metal frames should be deep red. Just a touch of color that makes the whole thing stand out. It doesn't get lost against the rest of the dark exterior."

"Thanks. I'm glad they liked it, even though it isn't modern. Craftsman-style windows did something like that in the 1920s." I walked around the side of the home and Mario followed.

"Hey, congrats again on your new nephew, by the way," he said. Mario had known my family for forever, so he was one of my first phone calls when baby James was born.

"Did you get any leads on the children's wing before you left the event?"

All the top people in my construction company knew what my plans were, and how I expected to grow the business over the next couple of years. We were all tasked with keeping our eyes open for any new opportunities that worked with the plan.

"Thanks, and I did meet someone. A doctor from the hospital."

"That's it? After spending a whole evening there?" Mario asked, surprise in his voice. "That's not like you—you've never met a stranger."

I shrugged. "I met a bunch of people. I'm just not sure any of them are going to be able to help me out."

Mario frowned at me. "Wait a minute. Who's the doctor?"

"What? I just said I met a bunch of people."

"But first you said you met someone. A doctor. Who was it? Did you meet a woman? You usually have a serious girlfriend, but it's been a while since the last one."

That was the problem when most of your life was spent on your business. Your personal life turned into business. Of course, Mario and I had known each other since we were kids, so I guess there could be worse problems.

"It's nothing. Just a doctor. And yes, she's a woman. I met her at the cooking class. Well, I kind of met her at the charity ball, but kind of not. We really met at the class."

Mario stopped walking and stood in place. I turned back to look at him.

"What cooking class? You don't need a cooking class—you're a great cook. And I should know—I've never missed one of your cookouts."

"It's nothing. Just a class I bought at the charity event's silent auction. It was for a good cause."

"But that's where you met the woman. The woman doctor, who you kind of met at the charity, but not really?" Mario asked, but it was more like a statement.

"Yep. You've got it."

"I know you need to get to the next site, but I won't forget about this. I'll expect to hear about it the next chance we get."

"There's nothing to tell, Mario, so no need to be waiting around for a story. There isn't one." We made our way back to the front of the site.

"I'll be the judge of that," he said. "Give me a call this weekend if you want to meet up. Now that there's a story you need to tell."

"There's not. And I can't. The cooking class will still be going on."

I don't know what he heard in my voice, but Mario reached out a hand and stopped me. "Wait, wait, wait. What aren't you telling me? Something's going on here."

I shook off his hand. "There's nothing. There's not. And I've gotta get to the next site." I walked quickly to my truck.

"Don't think you're getting out of this that easily, James. You'll be telling me all about it," he called and started to laugh.

I jumped in my truck and took off. The goodbye wave I tossed over my shoulder morphed into something rude.

I could still hear him laughing.

I didn't convince Mario there was nothing going on.

How would I convince myself?

Chapter 9

- Ellie

I was going to scream. No, wait. First I was going to kick something, and then I was going to scream. How freaking hard could it be to put together a set of bunk beds? Well, super hard, if my run at it was any indication.

The morning started off great. I was still on a high after the success of the cooking class. I mean, who knew that chocolate lava cake was so simple to make? And delicious, to boot. Of course, I was really thinking of James. I was just covering it up by thinking of the cake. And now I was thinking of covering up James with cake. My gosh, I needed to get my mind out of the gutter.

Before I went to bed last night, I'd made up my mind. I was going to take in EB, my sister's daughter. But temporarily. Just until a permanent home could be found for her. I had no intention of ever being a mother, not after the mother I had. I'd spoken with Mrs. Gonzales at Child Protective Services—CPS—again, this morning, and had set everything in motion.

The basic phone interview with her had gone well, especially when she'd found out I was a doctor and financially independent. Having the money to care for a child was always a concern, even though there would be a small stipend from the government. I let her know that that wouldn't be necessary, I'd be able to afford EB on my own. My bigger concern was finding her a permanent home.

An official interview was set up for the following week, downtown at the CPS offices. Between now and then they would do a background check as well as run my financials. I felt pretty good that those things were basically formalities. I was a doctor who made decent money. Things with CPS should go pretty smoothly.

Along with the interview and background check, we scheduled an in-home visit. My apartment had to be "child-ready"—words I never intended to apply to me. I was able to clean out the second bedroom, which I'd been using as an office, so I could set it up for EB's bedroom. It was a pain in the butt to move my desk and research items, but since I didn't have a ton of furniture, knick-knacks, or even a bed in that room that needed to be moved, it wasn't too bad. There was a corner in the living room that I could use, so I moved everything there.

I was happy with how things were progressing. Once I made up my mind about something, I stuck to it. Not unlike how I made my way through medical school, and how I was approaching the Tate Award.

So I was feeling pretty good, all the way up through finding bunk beds at a local store this morning, with a promise to deliver the beds by three this afternoon. Perfect. I even got to spend some much-needed time on my Tate project, where I finally delved deeper into some of the test results I was studying.

All of that came to a screeching halt with the arrival of the bunk beds. The two delivery guys brought the big box right into the bedroom, wished me luck, and went about their day. I'd already grossly underestimated just how big the box was that held the beds—it barely fit in the room. It was much worse once I cut it off the beds. What on earth was I going to do with all of this cardboard and plastic strapping that held everything together? I couldn't remember the last time I needed to dispose of something that didn't fit into a kitchen trash bag.

After I struggled for way too long, I managed to beat the box and straps into submission, as well as move it all into the living room. My apartment was filling up fast, and there wasn't even a child in it yet. I called maintenance and left a message about the cardboard, and then grabbed my toolbox.

I believed that every adult should have a toolbox, a fire extinguisher, and a first aid kit, and I was nothing if not prepared. The toolbox sat right next to my first aid kit in my linen closet, though a doctor's kit is a little bit different from what you pick up at the drugstore for first aid. Mine had a whole suturing kit, including needles and numbing agents. I'd never needed them at home, but better safe than sorry.

I laid out all of the pieces for the bed and grouped like things with like, in size order. It was like a giant-size version of the instrument tray I used during surgery. The first thing I noted was there were too many pieces. Hmmm. Well, better too many than not enough, so I got to work.

Three hours later, and I don't know if I'd ever been so frustrated in my life. This wasn't like delivering a baby, or even studying during med school. This was downright torture. It didn't matter what I tried, or how many times I went back to the so-called instructions. What I'd put together so far did not resemble the bunkbeds I saw in the store. And by no stretch of the imagination would this thing pass as safe.

What was I doing? I had less than an hour to get to cooking class, I had barely put in the time I needed for the Tate, and these beds were impossible. I was not cut out to be a mother, and here was more proof. I should stick to being a doctor. I'd have to call Mrs. Gonzalez tomorrow and... shoot. The offices were closed on the weekend. Well, I'd have to call her first

thing on Monday and let her know I couldn't do this. I just....
couldn't.

With that conclusion, I scrambled to get ready, then hurried
to cooking class.

"Dr. Ellie, you made it." James welcomed me warmly, which
I appreciated. I wasn't at all happy with the way the day had
ended up. I wasn't a quitter—like, at all, but I had to face
facts. I was the last person who was meant to be a mother to
someone.

I attempted a smile for James, but even I could tell it was
lackluster. It held no spark.

James's welcoming grin slid right off his face.

"What's wrong? Are you okay?"

So much for trying to return James's warm welcome.

James reached for my shoulder and gave it a small squeeze.
And for the first time in forever, I almost cried. What on earth?
I reached up to stop a tear before it started. I don't cry. I wasn't
going to start now, in front of James and the rest of the class.

There was a lot of excitement in the room while people
set up their stations and prepped for class, so I used the
commotion to duck down and pull out our cookware from the
cabinet. Totally effective in dodging James's questions.

"I'm good. Just been a crazy day."

I stood and mustered a more heartfelt smile for James. This
one actually reached the corners of my eyes.

I really was happy to see him.

He accepted my answer, though it was clear he didn't believe me. He wasn't the kind of guy to push; I liked that about
him. I found that I liked a lot of things about him.

I set the mixing bowls and measuring cups onto our cooktop. "What about you? How was your day?"

James's mouth slid into a smile. "It was excellent. The work sites are on schedule and on budget, which will free me up to pursue the hospital children's wing. I'm working on a plan to approach that more systematically. I like to have a good plan in place—things work more smoothly for me when I do."

Behind us, Brett and Shauna were all set up, and called out greetings, right as Chef Mike started the class.

"All right, everyone, welcome back to our *Lonely Hearts Club Cooking Class*, and hopefully some of you won't be lonely by the time it's over. We've got a big night ahead of us, so let's get to it. We're making two entrees and four sides tonight, so you can walk away from this experience feeling a lot better about what you're going to have for dinner next week, even if you don't have a new date. We're starting with Rosemary Garlic Pork Tenderloin and then we'll do a chicken dish. It's easy, delicious, and impressive. Remember, if you can't be impressive, at least your meals can be. Grab your recipe card, pull out your ingredients, and let's go."

James suggested we flip-flop our roles from the night before, so I got the ingredients together, while he grabbed specific bowls and measuring cups.

The first thing we needed to do was rough-cut the fresh rosemary, as well as chop an onion and garlic. I picked up one of the knives on the cooktop and began to chop the rosemary.

"Whoa, whoa, whoa, wait a minute Ellie, careful. Careful." James slowly reached for the knife and took it out of my hands. "How about I give you a little lesson on what knife to use and how to use it for chopping."

"What? What's wrong with what I was doing? I was totally chopping the rosemary."

Right about that time Chef Mike said, "My assistants will be available, so call on them, especially when using the Chef's Knife. It's easy once you see how to use it, and it'll make your experience in the kitchen that much better."

James gave me a little grin. "Doc, I can tell just by watching that you know how to use a scalpel, but this is different. Here, let me show you."

James nudged me aside from the cutting board, and I had to admit I lingered for a moment so I could stand there next to him, side to side. Not quite as good as the one-armed hug from last night, but I'd take it.

"You don't pick the knife up off the cutting board with every cut. What you want to do is rock the knife, back and forth over the top of the rosemary, without lifting the knife up. You secure the knife with your opposite hand, keeping your fingers up and away for safety."

James slowly rocked the knife back and forth over the rosemary, pivoting slightly with each cut as he made his way through the herb.

"You'll use this same technique when you chop the onion and the garlic too. And when you get really comfortable with it, you can go faster."

With that statement, James's knife practically blurred, and he finished cutting the rosemary almost as soon as he started.

"See? Like that. Now you try, with the garlic."

I gave James a bit of a squint. "You may be fast with a Chef's Knife, James Cross, but I can stitch you up quicker than a wink when you slice into one of your fingers with how fast you were going with that thing."

James threw his head back laughing, and I joined him. Maybe my day hadn't been such a bust after all.

"Hey, what's so funny?" Brett asked from behind us.

"Just Ellie. Making medical jokes at my expense."

Brett and Shauna both smiled at us, and James asked, "How is your prep coming along?"

"Good, I think." Shauna looked at Brett for confirmation. "We're both good in the kitchen, but we had one of the assistants give us a lesson on how to peel and chop the garlic cloves."

Chef Mike grabbed our attention and got everyone started on the next dish. I came back from the fridge with our cold ingredients, while James worked on a brine for the chicken.

"So, Ellie, how are you feeling?" James asked, and added salt to the water for the brine.

"Me? I'm good. Wait. Feeling about what? The cooking?"

James reached for the paprika. "Yeah, the cooking. And whatever else. You seem a bit distracted tonight."

I stood there and watched James mix up the brine, while I was slow to answer. Finally, I said, "Yeah, I've got a lot on my mind."

"Still thinking about the community service you need to do for that award? You know I said you could help us out with one of our projects if you wanted."

In between working on the Tate and getting things together with CPS, James had not been far from my mind. Maybe I should...

"James, can I ask you for a favor?"

James's head shot up.

"Of course."

And I could tell he meant it. So I just blurted it out.

"How would you like to help me get ready for a child?"

Chapter 10

- *James*

"What did you just say?" I could feel my eyes go round, taking over my face.

Ellie ran a hand through her hair, and I distractedly wished it was me doing that.

"A child. Help me get ready... wait. Not my child—I don't have any children. I won't be having any children. But my niece. EB."

Slowly I pushed aside the bowls I'd been working with. "Okay. What do you mean, help you get ready? Ready for what, exactly?"

She took a deep breath.

"My sister passed away, and her daughter needs a place to stay until a permanent home can be found for her."

I reached out for Ellie—it seemed like the natural thing to do— but I stopped right before my hand landed on hers. She stood so stiffly, so straight, I thought she might not want to be touched at all. "Ellie. I'm sorry. That's terrible. Are you okay? No wonder you didn't look like yourself when you came in tonight."

She tried to brush off my comment, but her mouth and eyes were pinched. "It's not that big of a deal—my sister and I weren't close. But I do feel bad for her daughter, and I decided I could help out by letting her stay with me for a while."

Not that big of a deal? What kind of relationship did she have with her sister? I couldn't even think of how I'd feel if my sister passed away and suddenly I was in charge of my new nephew, baby James.

"Of course, I'll help. Anything that you want."

Ellie let out a breath. "My apartment has to be 'child-ready,' according to Child Protective Services, and they'll be making a home visit soon. I thought I could manage things on my own, but all I've done so far is try to put the bunk beds together, and it's been a nightmare. Have you ever put together a set of bunk beds?"

I chuckled and shook my head. "I haven't. But I'd like to think I'm the perfect guy for the job, what with my building background. I'd be happy to help. Just tell me where and when."

A look of relief crossed Ellie's face. "Thank you. I'm used to doing things by myself, and I never thought it would be bunk beds of all things that would bring me to my knees. I can't thank you enough. Does tomorrow work for you?"

I couldn't just stand here doing nothing, because that wasn't me. This time, I did reach out to touch her and gave her another side hug like the one from the night before. A side hug with Ellie was becoming one of my favorite things.

"You're welcome. And tomorrow will be fine."

I let her go, and Ellie smiled, all the way to her eyes. "Ok. Tomorrow it is. Now let's get on with this meal—we don't want to fall behind. I don't think Chef Mike will approve of us getting trichinosis from undercooked pork."

I raised my eyebrows. "Trichinosis? I think you get 50 points for that word."

Ellie laughed and grinned. "Not when you're a doctor, you don't."

Class went by fast. Ellie seemed less stressed than she did when she got to class, and we were having fun together; with Shauna and Brett too. We got lucky to have the station right in front of them—we were all becoming fast friends. The other people in the class were great, like Nira and Jill who I met in yesterday's icebreaker, but something about the four of us felt real. Like we'd last beyond this classroom.

Best of all, everything we cooked tonight had been delicious. Ellie was coming along in the cooking department.

Chef Mike called our attention. "All right, we're going to end class with another opportunity to get to know your classmates. Grab your 'food that puts you in the mood' from yesterday, and let's meet up front."

Picking up his eggplant— his literal eggplant, not what it represented—Brett reached for Shauna's hand. "Come on Shauna, grab those tiny little figs of yours—which are an insult to all men everywhere, by the way—and let's see what Chef Mike has up his sleeve tonight."

I noticed the hand grab and Ellie gave me a quick look with raised eyebrows. Yeah, things were moving along for Brett and Shauna.

With my literal juicy peach and Ellie beside me with her banana, we moved through the workstations to the front of the class.

"Tonight we're going to start with Nira. Nira, what is your 'food that gets you in the mood?'"

I'd met Nira last night. She was a pretty, dark-haired woman, with beautiful deep brown eyes and tan skin. She held up a green, shiny cucumber.

One of the guys—his name tag said Jeff—said, "That's a great representation," and Nira actually blushed. The classroom laughed, and I glanced at Ellie to see if she was laughing, too. She was. And I felt my chest warm.

"Alright, everyone, I want you to call out any dishes you can think of that are made with cucumbers," said Chef Mike.

"Spicy cucumber salad from my favorite Chinese restaurant," said a woman named Kate.

"Greek tzatziki sauce," I called out.

"Anyone else have any ideas?" asked Chef Mike. "No? Okay, Nira, if you were going to pick, would you eat Chinese spicy cucumber salad or Greek tzatziki sauce?"

Nira scrunched up her nose and said, "I'd definitely go with tzatziki sauce. I don't like spicy things."

"Tzatziki sauce it is. James, please pair up with Nira," Chef Mike said, and I made my way over to stand next to Nira. I glanced over at Ellie, and she had a slight frown on her face.

"Kate, you're up. What do you have?" Kate held up an eggplant.

Brett called out, "Looks like we're a match, Kate," and held up his eggplant. The class burst out laughing, which was what Brett was going for.

"Okay, great. What can we make with eggplant?" asked Chef Mike.

"Eggplant parmesan," was called out by a classmate, and then "baba ghanouj" by Jamal. I recognized him as one of the men who was in Ellie's icebreaker group yesterday.

"Baba ghanouj, one of my favorites. Okay, Kate, which do you prefer?"

"Definitely baba ghanouj. I love it."

"Great. Jamal, pair up with Kate."

"What about me?" asked Brett. "You can't just leave me and my eggplant hanging." The class laughed, and Chef Mike replied. "Don't worry Brett. You and your big eggplant will get your turn."

We continued around the class with the icebreaker, until everyone had been paired up. Ellie ended up with the guy named Jeff, who had suggested banana bread for her banana, Brett was paired with Jill from my icebreaker group last night, and Shauna was matched with a man named Noah who had suggested a charcuterie board for her figs.

"Now that everyone is paired, spend some time with each other talking about why you picked the food that you picked. Why you like it, the best place you've ever had it, that kind of thing. And you know that old saying 'the way to a man's heart is through his stomach?' It applies to everyone. Cooking for someone, feeding someone, is an expression of love. You're literally helping someone stay alive by cooking for them. And you go beyond sustenance when you're cooking them something they love, or you love, whether it's your mom's famous meatloaf or a lobster and steak surf and turf. What better way is there to show that you care? So let's take a minute and talk about food."

While I enjoyed my discussion with Nira—it turned out she didn't even like cucumbers and she had never had tzatziki sauce—I kept looking across the room at Ellie, and wondered how she was doing.

Chef Mike wrapped up the class and reminded us all that tomorrow was our cooking and presentation competition. "You'll be cooking two things tomorrow. One entree, and one side, appetizer or dessert. You can prepare anything that you learned here, or you can make something of your own. If you're doing your own thing, you'll need to bring in your own supplies. Email me by four tomorrow afternoon so that we can get the ingredients needed for anything you learned here." He clapped his hands together. "Great class everyone. And remember, if you can't be intriguing, at least your meals can be! See you tomorrow night."

Ellie had made it clear she could be on the competitive side, so I thought we might have a shot at this competition.

"So what are you thinking in terms of the competition?" I asked as we cleaned up our workstation.

"Don't even think that you're going to win that thing, James," Brett said from behind us. "Shauna and I have it all wrapped up."

Ellie turned and gave him a look. "Really Brett? You have it all wrapped up? If you're so sure, how about you put your money where your mouth is. Let's bet."

"Whoa. I wasn't expecting that. Ok, Ellie, let's do it. What will it be? When Shauna and I win for best tasting dish, what will we win?"

Ellie smirked. "Simple. The losers have to pick up the food and drinks for our personal cooking class that James is going to host. And, they have to do all the clean-up, too."

Shauna laughed. Brett nodded his head and said, "Perfect. That's perfect. Since I know we're going to win, I can tell you now that I will thoroughly enjoy a relaxing evening of good food, good drink, and good company, without lifting a single finger to help. It'll be great."

Shauna nudged Brett on the shoulder. "Now look what you've done. We better win, Brett. I can't even tell you how much I hate doing dishes." Shauna laughed while she talked, but I think she meant it.

"Shauna, Shauna. Never fear. Let's head over to the pub and put together our devious plans. Ellie and James, care to join us?"

I turned to Ellie, but I knew she wouldn't. She had a lot on her mind.

"Thanks, guys, but I really can't. I've got to get home. But I'll see you here tomorrow night for the big cooking showdown."

Before Ellie could leave, I asked her if she'd like me to walk her to her car, but she declined. I knew she would—the girl had independence down to an art. We made plans to talk about the food competition tomorrow while I helped her with the bunk beds.

"Well, James, what about you? Want to join us?" Shauna asked.

It would be fun to join them, but Ellie didn't say anything to Shauna and Brett about the two of us getting together tomorrow, and I didn't think I could hang out with them without letting that slip. She seemed private, and I didn't want to lose any trust I'd gained over these past couple of days. I liked her. For real.

"Nah, you guys go ahead. That'll leave you free to come up with your nefarious plans. Plans that will do you no good, by the way, 'cause we're going to win."

We laughed and moved to exit. I was leaving the cooking class behind, but I had getting together with Ellie ahead.

I liked what my future held.

The question was—did Ellie?

Chapter 11

- Ellie

As I walked toward my car, I felt like I was leaving all of my happiness behind. And that was odd. I would typically describe myself as completely content with my life. Doing things *for* people made me feel good—it was one of the reasons I wanted to be a doctor—but just hanging out *with* people wasn't really my thing. I loved being alone and doing things on my own, yet now, walking away from this cooking class made me...melancholy? What was that all about?

I shook my head and tried to rid myself of the feeling. I reached for the car door. Something about the way I parked reminded me of the other night when my car had been stolen—and then returned—at the hospital. Such a weird, weird thing to happen. But I didn't feel any need to pursue the theft. I had my car, and everything was fine with it. I had far bigger things to worry about.

James for one. Well, he wasn't so much a worry. But he was most definitely on my mind. He'd be over first thing in the morning to help with the bunk beds. It wasn't like me to have asked him for help—I never asked for help. But I'd already wasted hours on the stupid bunk beds. I only had two days left of my scheduled time off, and I'd barely touched my research. I really needed to put in some quality time, or Dr. Butt-Kiss, I mean, Dr. Marks, would take the top prize, and that would not do. The Tate Award was mine, and I wouldn't let that schmoozer take it from me.

I stopped at the grocery store to grab a couple of things before James came over. James. There he was in my head again. When was the last time I had a guy over to my apartment? Wait. When was the last time I had anyone over to my apartment? Jasmine had come by a couple of months ago when I hadn't felt well—she was ever the nurse—but other than that, I couldn't remember the previous time. Aaaand now I felt melancholy again. If thinking about James was going to lead to these kinds of feelings, maybe I needed to get him out of my head for good.

I grabbed enough food and snacks to get through the next couple of days and walked out of the store when I got a text from Jasmine.

Jas: How is it that TWO SPLHCCC have finished and I haven't heard a word about it from you?
Me: Wait. What? SPLHCCC...??
Jas: Get with it Ellie. Srgt Pepper's Lonely Hearts Club Cooking Class .... SPLHCCC... all the cool kids are saying it.
Me: Ha! Of course they are. Class has been fine.
Jas: Fine? Class has been fine? That's all you got?
Me: Ok how about fun. Class has been fun.
Jas: Well knock me over. Fun. That's practically shouting from the rooftops for you. I expect to hear all about it. And I do mean ALL about it when you're back at work on Monday.
Me: I'd expect nothing less. Talk then.
Jas: Byeeeee

Thank God for Jasmine. I could always count on her to lift my spirits. I threw my groceries into the backseat and promised myself that tomorrow would be fine, and I wouldn't let James get me all melancholy again. I'd kick him out as soon as the bunk beds were built, and get back to work on my research. Perfect.

Not perfect. I sat at my desk, supposedly getting some research in tonight, and all I could think about was James. James during our cooking classes. James coming over tomorrow. James and his side hugs. James, James, James. What is wrong with me? *Really, Ellie, get a hold of yourself.* It was so not like me to be... mooning over a guy. No other guy I ever went out with made me feel this way. I dated them until I didn't. And that was that. And that's the way I liked it. No promises, no commitments, no expectations. Getting close to someone meant someone getting close to me, and that would be bad for everyone involved.

I was clear about what I wanted out of a relationship—the bare minimum. I was very upfront about it. James was a nice guy who had agreed to help me out of a jam. That was it. That's where he'd stay.

I pushed back from my desk and took a quick walk around the room. I tried to clear my head. I didn't mind having my work desk in the main living space. Though my place wasn't what you would call decorated, having my desk out with the couch and TV made it feel a little bit more like there was actually life here. That someone lived here, didn't just sleep here.

I paused and took a look around the room. Oh my gosh, it was barren. Not a single piece of art, not a single framed photograph, only the barest of necessities. I'd never cared about any of that. Stuff was just stuff. When you moved from foster home to foster home, stuff was just a burden. Or someone was going to take it away from you in the end, anyway, so why bother.

But there was my plush throw blanket folded over the back of the sofa. I couldn't resist it after I saw it over and over when I surfed the shopping channels. I could remember the exact day that I bought the sofa, and this throw was perfect for it. Perfect for the many nights I knew I would end up crashing on the sofa. In fact, that sounded like an even better idea than trying to get some work done. So I snuggled under the blanket, flipped on the TV, and tried to erase James from my mind.

Was that knocking? And why was there so much light in my room? I always closed my blackout curtains before I went to bed. Those things were imperative, especially in the middle of the day when I'd worked an overnight shift. So why was there so much light...

Oh, shoot. James was here.

Chapter 12

- James

I slept like garbage last night. I guess it was from being amped up in cooking class. I hadn't been able to fall asleep.

First, I watched a bunch of videos on how to put together bunk beds. I was being ridiculous. I knew I could build bunk beds from scratch. But I wanted to impress Dr. Ellie—well, Ellie—and I didn't want to look like a fool who had to ask for the instructions on how to put together the beds. Everybody knew you didn't need instructions. Satisfied that I'd seen every and all variations on how to assemble the beds, I moved on to my laundry.

Yes, I did need to do my laundry. But I lost my man card when I stood in my closet and inventoried my clothes, thinking about what I'd wear over to Ellie's. Like it was a date. Not just a date, but a very important date that took forethought and planning in regards to what I would wear.

Now don't get me wrong. I always put thought into my dates. The women I take out deserve that kind of respect. All women deserve that respect. But this wasn't a date. This wasn't a date at all. This was helping a woman—an attractive, smart, funny woman who seemed very private—out of a tough spot. So why was I in my closet, searching for "date" clothes?

I was concentrating on building my business right now. Not on getting into another relationship that would fade into nothing.

I decided I would wear a t-shirt, jeans, and work boots, exactly what you would think your non-date builder friend—were we friends? We were friends—would wear to help you build something. It was the second time that night I found myself being ridiculous.

Then I tried to figure out what I could bring to her house the next day and even considered baking my mom's incredible cinnamon roll recipe, so I could bring it for breakfast.

Clearly, I was out of my mind. She had *just* invited me over to help. There weren't that many hours between the end of class and going to her apartment, but somehow I was casually going to work in making her homemade rolls? Ridiculous. Ridiculous. Ridiculous.

I ended up in jeans and a t-shirt with coffee and muffins I picked up on the way over. And they had to be chocolate. I saw how much she loved that molten lava cake we made in class.

Dr. Ellie's apartment building was understated but in a nice part of town. Someone was walking out, so I didn't need to buzz in, and I went straight to her door. I don't know what I expected, because the truth was I really didn't know much about her. That was becoming quite clear to me as I stood in front of her door and knocked for the second time. We did say 8:00 am sharp, right?

The door jerked open, and there she stood, looking... a lot like she looked the night before. Maybe exactly like the night before, with the same clothes and same hair...but messier. Still adorable. Dang it.

I held up the tray of coffees in front of me. "Coffee?"

"Good gosh, yes," she said and reached for the tray. She opened the door wider. "Come in, come in. I'm so sorry,

I fell asleep on the couch last night and overslept. I never oversleep."

I stepped into her apartment, and even though I didn't know her well, there was nothing in her apartment that was going to help me get to know her better because anyone could have lived there. There wasn't a single personal thing that I could see at first glance. Just living room furniture and a TV, an office desk in the corner, and a big blanket lying half on the sofa and half on the floor.

I stepped toward the kitchen and eat-in area and set down the bag of muffins on the small table there.

"Hey, what else did you bring?" she asked.

"I took a guess, based on how much you liked the molten lava cake we made the other night. So I got double chocolate muffins from the coffee shop."

"Thank you," she said. "You didn't have to, but I'm so glad you did. I bought groceries and was going to make you some eggs and bacon as a thank you, but oversleeping ruined that plan."

"That's okay. My mom—and my sister—would kill me if I didn't show up with something, so I'm doubly glad I brought them now. And besides," I said while I raised an eyebrow, "I know you're not much of a cook."

Luckily, she laughed at that remark, rather than get offended.

"True, so true," she said while taking a sip of coffee and opening up the muffins. "But eggs and bacon, I can do."

"You'll have to make them for me the next morning we're together then," I said, and immediately wanted to take my foot out of my mouth. The next morning we're together? Like we're going to make this a regular thing? Or worse, did I imply I'd be sleeping over? Not that that would be the worst thing, but heck. What had I just said?

She shot me a look over her shoulder from where she had moved to the kitchen cabinets to grab some small plates and napkins, but she didn't acknowledge the comment beyond that. "Do you want a mug to pour your coffee in, or are you good with the to-go cup?"

I was relieved that she didn't say anything about my awkward statement, and I quickly replied. "I'm good. Moving between job sites, my coffee is almost exclusively in to-go cups. I'm good with this."

"I'm the same with my work at the hospital. It's always coffee to go. Which is why when I have the chance, I try to drink it from a mug. One of the few times I actually slow down." She grabbed a mug with the other things, and then we both sat down at the table.

I reached into the bag and placed a muffin on her plate, while she popped the lid off her coffee and poured it into her mug. She sat back in her chair and took a big bite of muffin.

"So you never slow down?" I asked while I reached for my own muffin.

"Wow, these are good," she said. "Thanks again, for bringing them."

"No problem."

"So yeah, mostly I work. Like, all the time. And if I'm not working, I'm working on things related to work. Like that research I'm doing right now. One of the reasons I don't cook. It's easier to just get delivery or grab something at the hospital and less disruptive to my work."

"Ah. I can see that. I have the same problem. I can spend all my time working, too. So I use cooking to slow down. If I promise a bunch of people I'm going to cook for them, that forces me to stop working, and spend some real time with my friends or family."

She gave a little laugh and said, "Oh, you misunderstood. It's not a problem that I'm working all the time. I love my work. I'd much rather be working than being forced into quality time with... well, just about anyone."

She pushed back from the table and grabbed our empty plates. "Would it be rude if I hopped in the shower real quick? The bunk beds are in the room down the hall to the left. When I'm done I'll join you."

She left me at the table, where I puzzled over her statement about being forced into quality time and tried really hard not to think about joining her in the shower.

Chapter 13

- Ellie

I was in the shower, while a man I barely knew was just down the hall. What was I thinking? And what must he be thinking...of me? What kind of woman announces I'm going to take a shower and then... oh my gosh. Did he think that was an invitation? Some kind of invitation to—well, it could be all sorts of things, but really. Who does that?

I jumped out of the shower, and quickly pulled my hair up on top of my head in a messy bun. I flung open my closet door and reached for—what exactly? A t-shirt? Jeans? James had on a t-shirt and jeans. Mighty fine looking t-shirt and jeans for a mighty fine looking... wait a minute. We'd be working around the house, that's what I'd dress for.

After I pulled on my clothes, I jogged out of my room and yelled "I'm coming, I'm coming," as I went down the hall. I grabbed the doorframe into the bedroom and slid into the room.

James was crouched in the middle of the floor, and I swear the bunk beds were half-built. "Whoa," I said, and took in the room. "How did you do that so fast? I couldn't have been gone for more than 15 minutes."

James smiled as he turned toward me, and the smile grew even broader when he saw me. "Whoa, yourself. You look nice."

"What, this old thing?" We both laughed at the line. Apparently, the two seconds of extra thought I put into getting dressed paid off. I wore cut-off jean shorts that I paired with my favorite pale pink v-neck long-sleeved tee. It was perfect for what we were working on, and it fit. Nicely.

"Thanks. I was trying to go for something other than the scrubs I wear to work.... and for that matter the scrubs I wear at home, too. Hmm. Plus I have company, so..."

James stood up. "I'm company?"

"You are definitely company—you brought coffee and muffins. And now you've done, like, everything."

James glanced around the room. "Not exactly everything. I'll need a little help from you getting these top supports up, but then comes the tedious, pain in the butt part."

"And what is that?" I looked around the room. The beds did seem almost put together.

"See that big pile of nuts and bolts?" He pointed to a pile of parts pushed over by the side of the room.

I squinted while I glanced at the pile. "Yeah. When I was trying to put this thing together yesterday—and failing miserably—I decided that those parts were 'extra.' You know, extra stuff in case you lost something." I smiled when I said it, so he would know I didn't really think that, but I really did kind of think that.

James laughed. "It's not typical for them to give you extras. Just for future reference."

"Oh, hold on. I am never building anything again. This is it. Basically one and done."

"Alright. Well in the meantime, in order to finish these beds, after we get the upper level up, we need to secure the brace bars to the backside and then tighten those extra nuts and bolts into every one of those holes you see running along the frame. It's a pain in the butt because there are a ton of them. And you can't skip them—it's what makes the whole bed set-up safe."

"Ah. So the extras are for safety. Noted." I smacked my hands lightly on my thighs. "Okay then. Put me to work."

- James

Helping Ellie out was...fun. For starters, she looked—and smelled—incredible, even though she wasn't wearing anything special, just a t-shirt and shorts. Simple enough to show off her slim curves, which I could appreciate. I could always find something attractive about a woman, but there was something special about Ellie.

Working on the bunk beds as a team was also easy, like when we were cooking together. We had gotten the upper sides in place and began to clean up some of the packaging, mainly to get it out of our way, when Ellie reached for the instruction booklet buried under some plastic.

"Hey," she said, pulling the papers free from the pile. "I know you're a builder and all, but really, you didn't pick up the instructions once?"

There was no way I was going to tell her about the videos I'd watched the night before. So I shrugged.

"Nah. I build homes for a living. Building a set of bunk beds is nothing."

"You know, I really thought I would be able to put these things together by myself," she said. "But even following the instructions—which I would claim were completely useless—I couldn't figure out why certain pieces were supposed to go together. But it became clear once I was building it with you."

We were both kneeling on the floor, screwing in nuts and bolts to make sure the bunks were secure. It took forever like I said it would. What I hadn't said was I could've gone down to my truck and brought up my electric cordless driver and hex heads, which would have cut down on the time we spent manually screwing in bolts by half. But why would I do a thing like that?

"I think it's like a lot of things," I said. "You can read about it, like in the instruction manual, but it's not until you see it being done that it really clicks."

"True. It was the hands-on experience when I worked with other doctors on rotations during med school that showed me I wanted to get into obstetrics. Including surgery. Performing surgery is a world away from reading about how to perform surgery."

"Did you always know you wanted to be a doctor?"

Ellie chuckled. "No. I wouldn't say that. It was more that I always knew what I didn't want to be."

"Yeah? And what was that?"

"Anything that my mother was."

Before I could respond to that unexpected answer, Ellie looked around the room.

"So that's it? We're finished? I don't see any more extra parts lying around." She was changing the subject and I was still so surprised by her response that I let it go.

"Yep, that's it. Now just help me wrestle these mattresses onto the bunks, and you'll be all set."

"Well, finally," she said. "It's lunchtime already. I had no idea this would take the whole morning. I thought two hours, max."

"Ah, a little tip from the building trade. When you're going to tackle a home improvement project, decide how long you think it is going to take. And then, no matter what, double it. That's how long it's really going to take."

Ellie laughed. "If this whole bunk bed situation is anything to go by, I believe you. Okay, let's get those mattresses in."

We slipped the mattresses into place and stepped back to admire our handiwork.

And that's when Ellie said, "Oh, shoot. This isn't done at all."

Chapter 14

- Ellie

I couldn't believe it. I'd worked hard getting my apartment ready for EB, and here I was, standing with James with the bunk beds all put together, and not one single sheet, blanket, or pillow for the beds. I hated that I overlooked that. It was like an obvious sign that I shouldn't be taking care of a child. And I didn't need to be thinking that way. I'd made the decision to temporarily take EB in, and that was what I was going to do. I'd already done enough flip-flopping in my mind.

"Ugh, I can't believe this. I forgot to get any bedding for the beds. And now that the bunk beds are set up, it's obvious I need to get a dresser and a little side table too. And a lamp. And what else? What else am I not thinking of?"

By this point, I think I sounded a little panicked.

Maybe because I felt a little panicked.

James reached out and placed his hand on my shoulder, and gave it a little squeeze.

"Whoa. It's okay, it's just some bedding. And a few things to finish out the room. We can make that happen, easy. Come on, let's grab a pen and paper, and put together a list. You got this."

James slid his hand down my arm and took my hand in his. Then he led me out of the room and over to my desk in the corner of the living room. He dropped my hand and pulled a piece of paper from the printer, and grabbed a pen. I admit I was disappointed he dropped my hand. I liked the comfort. His comfort.

"Alright. Let's brainstorm. What all do you need before you get your niece? You already said bedding. So sheets. A blanket or comforter. Pillows. And a dresser, side table and lamp. That all falls under the bedroom heading. What else might she need?"

I paced the room, while wave after wave of memories of being in foster care washed over me. What else might she need? Everything. Clothes, maybe some toys or a stuffed animal, kids' books, food. And safety. She needed to feel safe. That panicky feeling was back. I paced even more quickly and threw my hands around.

"She needs everything, James. Everything. I don't have any idea what it's been like living with my sister these past years, and she's going to be scared. Everything in her life has just changed. Everything. I don't know what she has or doesn't have, and believe me, I know how hard it is to ask for what you need or want from virtual strangers. And that's what I'll be to her. A stranger."

James stepped in front of me and took both of my hands in his, stopping my pacing.

"Ellie. It'll be okay. Just breathe. Take a big breath in, and slowly let it out. " James looked me right in the eye, and it was the best thing that could have happened. That was, until he dropped my hands, put his arms around me, and hugged me.

That was the best thing that could have happened.

- James

She was shaking. Ellie was physically shaking. I didn't know everything that was going on with her, but it was big, whatever it was. I kept one arm around her lower back, and slowly smoothed my other hand up and down her spine. "Just keep taking deep breaths. In, and out. In, and out."

After a few moments, I could feel the tension ease a bit from her shoulders, and she stepped back, then ran her hands over her face.

"Thank you. For the hug. I was starting to freak out."

She sounded surprised at herself, like any kind of emotional outburst didn't happen very often.

"Taking in your niece is a big deal. It would be a big deal for anyone. But in the short time I've known you, I get the feeling you can handle just about anything." I sat down on the sofa and patted the seat next to me. "Sit. Let's take a second."

"Let me just grab a water," she said. "You want one?" I knew this was a delay tactic, but she could take a minute to pull herself together if she needed to.

"Sure, grab me one too."

Ellie walked into the kitchen, and I heard her turn on the sink and wash her hands, and then open the fridge for the bottles of water. She was back in the living room in a few moments and plopped down on the sofa while she handed me my water.

She took a deep breath, and let it out. "So I'm guessing you want to know what that was all about."

I turned on the sofa, so I faced her more directly. I didn't want to pressure her, but I did want to know.

"Yeah, if you want to tell me. But you don't have to. I can see why realizing you forgot a whole list of things would stress you out."

Ellie lifted her leg up onto the sofa and put her head down. She pulled at the threads at the hem of her cut-off shorts.

"Well, it was the list," she said. "But it wasn't the list." She looked up at me then. "I spent eight years in foster care so I know exactly what this can do to a kid."

I tried to keep the surprise off my face, and just let her speak. I knew a couple of things about foster care, too, but this was not the time to bring that up. This was about her.

"My mom died of an overdose when I was ten and my sister was six. We barely knew our dad—he had skipped out on us before my sister had even turned one. And we didn't have any family to step in and help. Let me just say, that having everything in your world suddenly change, even when your world wasn't so great to begin with, is not a good thing. And getting ready for my niece is bringing it all back. She's just a year older than my sister was when our mom died."

"Wow. That's a lot. I can see why you're shaken up. But you just said you didn't have any family to take you in. So this is different. You're her family."

"Family she doesn't know, so I'm still a stranger in her eyes." Ellie was rubbing her temples by this point. "I don't know what I am thinking, taking her in. I'm as much of a stranger as anyone else. I bet there are other people out there better prepared to take her in until a more permanent foster home can be found."

I scooted over closer to Ellie, reached out again, and took her hands from her temples.

"Ellie, that might not be true," I said. "There's a very good chance your sister has talked about you, has told her things about you, about the two of you when you were growing up. You might be a stranger, but there's a chance that she knows some things about you. Which is more than she will know about anyone else out there. So if you're willing to do this, you really are the best bet for her."

She looked me in the eye again, and it was as if her whole soul was reflected there. In our short time together I had not seen her appear so vulnerable. Or more beautiful. What was it about this girl?

She pulled her hands from mine and reached up to undo and redo the pile of hair on top of her head.

My stomach dropped when she moved away. *Shoot. I had it bad*.

"I do want to do this. You're right. I am the best bet. Okay, then, let's get back to that list."

She stood up and walked over to the desk where I'd left the paper and pen. I had questions for her, but she was done talking. I was sure if she hadn't had that little meltdown right in front of me, I wouldn't have found out what I did about her past. Or at least it would have taken a lot longer for her to share.

And now I found I wanted to know... *everything*.

Chapter 15

- *Ellie*

The room was spinning around me. I leaned against the desk and held the list of things I needed for EB in my hand, but I wasn't seeing it. I saw all the ways that I could fail her. If I wasn't careful, the ledge that James had talked me off would appear again. And had I really just shared all of that about myself with him? And why did I want to tell him even more?

Deep breaths. I would continue to take deep breaths.

I turned to James. "Food. Food would be helpful at this point. Do you have time to stay for lunch, and we can continue to work on this list?" *Please say yes. Please say yes.*

James stood from the sofa and smiled. "Yep. I just need to check on a build later this afternoon, before cooking class. You know, you have a lot on your plate, so would it be helpful if I just took care of our plan for the cooking competition tonight? Or would you like the distraction? I know you like to win." There was something about the way he teased me that almost sounded like admiration.

"Actually, I'd love a distraction." I felt my shoulders and face start to relax. I took one of those much-needed deep breaths. "How about we order in, and go over the plans for getting ready for EB and for cooking class tonight. Figure out everything that needs to happen and go from there."

"Sounds great. First, lunch. What's good around here?" James looked at me expectantly. "I know you know the good stuff."

"I do. I definitely do. What do you like?" I was surprised I didn't know this since food and cooking were the basis of our relationship.

"I'm always good with pizza if you are."

"Yep. There's a great Italian, wood-fired grill place right around the corner, and they deliver. We can even order in- dividual pizzas." I stepped into the kitchen and grabbed the takeout menu from the junk drawer, then handed it to James.

"And I'm buying," I said. "You've been such an incredible help to me. Thank you, James."

"You're welcome. And I accept your pizza offering. I'm glad I could help. I think it's great what you're doing for EB."

"Well—"

"Oh, hey," James interrupted. "You never did say. Why did you decide to go with bunk beds? Putting together a single bed would've been much easier for you."

I'd already revealed so much to James. Why was it so easy to share things with this guy? Other than Jasmine, no one knew as much about me as he knew now. And if this kept up, he was about to know more. It felt good to say it all out loud, but I wasn't sure I was ready for that. I was afraid I'd say too much.

"First, the pizza. Then, the plans. Then we'll go from there."

James gave me a look like he knew exactly what I was doing—avoiding the question. And since he was absolutely right, I made no comment, I just reached for the phone to place our order.

- James

Getting personal information out of Ellie was harder than getting rusty nails out of an old piece of wood house framing. Every detail she told me made me want to hear more. Her unwillingness to open up made sense to me, but she had no idea how much I understood. To have gone through the things that she had at such a young age, and to end up a successful doctor was outright impressive. There was definitely something special about her.

We finished putting together the shopping list for EB when the pizza arrived.

I went to the door to buzz the delivery up, while Ellie got bottles of water out of the fridge. I got the pizza and set the boxes down on the eat-in kitchen table, then walked over to the sink to wash my hands. Ellie put the water on the table and joined me at the sink. She gave me a little hip bump so she could elbow her way in.

"Hey, I was here first. Wait your turn, lady," I joked, and gave her a little hip bump back. And then she completely surprised me by flicking water up in my face.

I jerked back reflexively, and she stepped right up to the faucet, shooting me a grin over her shoulder. "I think you meant, 'ladies first,'" she said and lathered up. I laughed.

"You're right. Where are my manners? By all means, go ahead." I leaned against the counter next to the sink and just stood there watching her. I didn't even care that I was being obvious. I was enjoying myself.

"So," I said. I took in her elaborate hand washing technique. "Do you always wash your hands as though you're scrubbing in for surgery?"

She laughed. "It's habit, at this point. I'm not a germaphobe or anything, but I do know what can live on your hands. I might as well wash my hands thoroughly since I'm about to pick that pizza up and put it directly in my mouth."

After that comment, I was no longer interested in her hand-washing at all, but much more interested in her mouth.

I gave myself a mental shake. My mind did not need to go there.

Ellie stepped back and grabbed a hand towel, and I cleared my throat and moved up to the sink to finish washing my hands. By the time I joined Ellie at the table, she had pulled out paper plates and napkins from the bag on top of the pizza boxes and was flipping open the lid on the top box.

"Fresh mozzarella and basil for you," she said and slid the box my way. "And meat lovers for me." She pulled the bottom box towards herself, opened it up, and took a slice.

"Meat lovers? You surprised me, that's not what I expected you'd order."

"No? Why not?" She looked up at me while she took a big bite of her pizza.

"I don't know. Maybe because even when a lot of girls say 'let's order pizza,' they order a salad. Or maybe a pepperoni. But I don't see a lot of meat lovers."

"Oh. Well, um, it kind of goes back to the foster care thing. There weren't a lot of meals with meat, 'cause you know, it's expensive. So when I had a little money of my own, an easy way to get meat was to get a slice of pizza with everything on it." She continued to eat her pizza, while I tried not to sit there dumbfounded. It was clear that no imagining on my part was going to match the reality of what she went through in the foster care system.

"And the bunk beds?" I asked. "I'd like to have a big family someday, so I'm all about it. But you don't sound like that's what you're preparing for here." I knew foster care could be bad for some kids, but had her experience been so awful she didn't ever want a family? That was just…sad.

"Well, you know I thought I could build them. In fact, I was sure I could, or I never would've gone with them. I prefer to take care of things myself."

"I like that about you. But, if you hadn't gone with the bunk beds, we wouldn't have had this time together, either." I gave Ellie what I hoped was a charming smile. "So why bunk beds?"

She took a deep breath. "It's silly, really. But when I was growing up, kids were always having sleepovers. Or even slumber parties. But when you're in foster care, you're often in a home with other foster kids or kids of the family that took you in. The environment doesn't lend itself to bringing another kid into the mix, even just for the night. At least in my experience."

I ate my pizza while I listened attentively. I didn't want to interrupt her while she was in the mood to share.

"And the truth is, I didn't really have any friends to invite over anyway. But I sure wanted them. If EB has friends, I want her to be able to invite them over for a sleepover."

And now I wanted to hug her again. She wasn't showing any signs of distress like earlier, but I felt it. My stomach twisted in knots for this woman, and the girl she used to be.

Ellie wiped her hands on a napkin and said, "Okay. What are we going to do about our competition tonight?"

Like she had done so many times before, she changed the subject.

But I was on to her.

I could be patient.

I was going to learn everything about Ellie Dumont.

Chapter 16

- Ellie

"You are definitely the better cook," I said. "And I really want to beat Shauna and Brett tonight in the competition. So, what do you think? How should we do this?"

James looked at me with a grin and chuckled. "Don't sell yourself short—you're really coming along."

I gave him a little bow. "Thank you. And it's good timing too. I'd like to be able to feed EB something other than what I ate through most of my childhood. Peanut butter."

James didn't make any comment about the peanut butter, which I was glad about. There was enough talk about my past. I was happy to be moving on.

"Let's go with a chicken dish, then," he said. "It's a safe bet for kids, and it can make enough for two meals. And how about we use one of my easy recipes, so you can have another meal to add to your cooking class collection."

"Can we win with that recipe? 'Cause you know, gotta beat Brett and Shauna." I raised my eyebrows.

He just laughed at me. "You are hardcore when it comes to competition. Yes, the meal is easy and delicious—I think Chef Mike will like it. So we'll have to get groceries for that. What about the side dish or dessert? You thinking anything special?"

"Hmm..." My mind immediately went to the chocolate lava cake we made the first night of class. It was so good and pretty easy, too.

"I love the thought of the chocolate lava cake. But if I'm trying to add to my recipes, what do you think? You have anything kid-friendly to suggest?"

"Chocolate chip cookies. Everyone loves them, and EB can even help you make them." He looked down for a moment like he was suddenly shy. "But I can teach you how to make cookies any time. We don't have to do that in class."

Oh, this guy. What was so special about James, that it was like I was falling for him? And falling for him fast. I hadn't fallen for a guy in... well, forever. I already liked him, and then that hug. It was...unexpected. And what I needed, when I didn't even know that was what I needed.

I held his gaze. "I'd like that." I waited for a beat before I broke the eye contact.

"So, the lava cake?" I asked.

"Yeah, let's do the lava cake. How about you email Chef Mike we're doing that and our own entree, and I'll pull up the chicken recipe and see what we need for groceries."

"Sounds good. And James?"

James glanced up from his phone. "Yeah?"

"Thanks for everything. For real." I wanted to say a lot more than that. I wanted to tell him how much having him with me—not just because of the bunk beds, but especially during my mini panic attack— meant to me. But I couldn't find the words.

"Yeah, Ellie, of course." James gave me a half smile and went back to work on our grocery list, while I emailed Chef Mike.

Because James still had to get to his work site, and I knew I could get the things I needed for EB tomorrow, we decided to pick up the groceries together. Then James would head out from there, so I could try to get something done on my Tate research.

I didn't think I'd ever shopped in a grocery store with a man before, and perhaps had never even thought about it, but it was a good experience with James. I found that I liked lots of experiences with James. Cooking together, building together, planning together. I'd done everything on my own for so long, that sharing in things, even the little things like picking up groceries struck a chord with me I didn't expect.

There was another thing I didn't expect. I liked James. I really liked James.

I had pulled up to my desk to try to get some work done on the Tate when Jasmine texted.

Jas: Hey girl. Dying to hear how the cooking class is going. Are you still burning Ramen to the bottom of the pan? Not sure how you even DO that?

Me: Thanks for the reminder and no. No burning Ramen. I think I've mastered a chocolate lava cake, though.

Jas: For reals? That sounds awesome. But before I forget, MARKS was asking about you yesterday. He was all - where is she, what is she doing - blah blah. I told him he could kiss my ...BUT I really don't care about him - see what I did there?! Ha! HOW ARE THE GUYS???

Me: Ha! Stupid Marks. And of course you want to hear about the guys! They're... Fine.

Jas: Don't give me that fine stuff El!

Me: Ok ok the class is good. For reals. I'll tell you all about it on Monday.

Jas: Monday? Monday! Monday is forever away. I need info now. Now Ellie. Don't leave me hanging.

Jas: Ellie? Ellie?

Jas: *You're doing it, aren't you. You're leaving me hanging.*
Jas: *Ellie?*
Jas: *Ok, Monday. You'll tell me EVERYTHING MONDAY!*
Me: :)

There was so much I needed to tell Jasmine. Not just about cooking class and James, but about EB, too. I hadn't even mentioned that I had a niece, and now here I was planning on temporarily fostering her. We'd have to talk on Monday.

I glanced at my phone and saw I had less than two hours to get two days' worth of research done, so I put my mind to it and got to work...right after thinking that it also meant I only had around two hours until I was going to see James again.

It couldn't get here soon enough.

Chapter 17

- James

What was this woman doing to me? I'd barely known her for three days, I'd spent more time with her today than I had with any other woman in months, and I was counting the minutes until I saw her again. Thank goodness we had another cooking class tonight, or I didn't know when I might see her again.

And I didn't like the thought of that at all.

After I swung by the job site—where everything looked good and Mario wasn't around to ask any more annoying questions—I decided to stop by my parent's house before I headed home and cleaned up for cooking class. My sister was staying with them for a while, and I wanted to get my hands on baby James.

I pulled up to my childhood home. Once this area was the suburbs, but urban sprawl had taken it over. On the one hand, it was great to have the restaurants and the conveniences of the city right at our fingertips here. On the other hand, I missed the wide-open spaces you used to see. I didn't think there was a single field left that we used to play in as kids. Thank goodness my parents' place backed up to a big green-way—at least it still felt like they lived in the country.

After I parked in the driveway of the sprawling two-story house, I made my way inside. I was quiet while I let myself in—I didn't want to wake the baby if he was asleep.

Sure enough, my sister Elizabeth sat in a glider chair, sleeping baby cradled in her lap, while she gently rocked back and forth.

"James. You're here," she said. "And perfect timing, too. Come get this little guy. If I don't get to the bathroom he's not the only one who will have wet pants. But wash your hands first—new human and all."

I stepped around the corner to the powder room and washed my hands, grabbed a hand towel to dry them, then walked back into the living room over to Lizzy. I reached down and carefully picked up James, being sure not to wake him. "You wetting your pants is more information than I needed Lizzy, way more. You can keep those details to yourself." I glanced around the room. "Where's mom?" I asked.

"She's in the kitchen, putting together some snacks. I eat almost as often as the little guy does. Breastfeeding literally takes it out of you." She quickly walked past me on the way to the bathroom and gave me a little bump on the shoulder. "Was that more information than you needed, brother?" She laughed as she made her way out of the room.

I shook my head at Lizzy, then looked down at baby James. He had changed so much. It had been one week since he was born, and he was already different. He was definitely bigger. I'd spent the whole day with him the day after he was born, and I was surprised at the changes a week brought.

Mom walked into the room, carrying a tray with cheese, crackers, some meats, and some fruits. "Hi, son." She set the tray down on the coffee table, stood up on her tiptoes and gave me a kiss on the cheek. She was a little thing, my mom.

"Hi, Mom," I said, while I tipped baby James towards her. "I can't believe how much he has changed in just a week."

"I know, it's amazing. I'm so grateful he and Lizzy can be here, but oh, Theo is missing so much."

Lizzy's Air Force pilot husband, Theo, was overseas, and he wouldn't be home for at least six more weeks.

"He is, but you know Lizzy is taking photos and videos every chance she gets. And if his first week is anything like his first day, he's probably just been sleeping a lot, right?"

Mom laughed. "So true. That baby is a sleeping machine. I think even your sister is getting sleep."

"Talking about me?" Lizzy asked, coming back to the room, and headed right for the cheeseboard. She flopped down next to Mom on the sofa and reached for the platter, so I made my way to the glider.

"We were. But really, we were talking about this good-looking baby of yours. And how much those good looks resemble me."

A small piece of cheese hit me in the side of the head and bounced onto the floor.

"Hey, careful—there's a baby here," I said and tried not to laugh.

"He looks exactly like Theo, and you know it. And I can't wait for him to get home and meet him," Lizzy said. She got comfortable on the sofa. "So where have you been all day? We thought you'd be over earlier."

That was the question I dreaded. I wasn't sure what I wanted to reveal about Ellie. We were just getting to know each other, and yet I'd spent the whole day with her. I didn't want to get into a whole big discussion about her. I definitely wasn't ready to tell them she delivered baby James.

"I just had some things to take care of. I had to run by a job site, and pick up some groceries for my cooking class tonight."

"Oh, your cooking class. The Dr. Pepper thing," my mom said. "How's it going?"

I laughed out loud, but quietly. "Sgt. Pepper's, Mom. And it's good. Chef Mike is great, and I've learned a couple of new recipes."

I hoped that would be enough information.

It wasn't.

Lizzy chimed in like I knew she would. "And the women? You did say it was a singles thing. Meet anyone nice?"

I took a deep breath. How much would I reveal? I liked Ellie, but I didn't want to get their hopes up. I'd disappointed them with my relationships in the past.

"Yeah, a couple of nice girls. My partner Ellie is pretty cool. And Shauna is the woman behind our station, and she's nice," I replied.

"Wait. Ellie is pretty 'cool'? Is that code for something? Since when do you call girls 'cool?'" Lizzy reached for more crackers from the tray.

I couldn't get away with anything with these two. "Right. Not cool. She's... smart. And competitive. And.... different." I paused and thought of how to better describe Ellie, when my sister sat up straight, her back lifting away from the sofa.

"What do you mean, 'different?' 'Different' how?" Lizzy planted her feet flat on the floor and shot my mom a look. My mom had her eyes open wide, and her mouth firmly shut. Oh, shoot. Nothing good was going to come out of this conversation.

"She's just... I don't know, different."

"Wait. Have you been with her today? Is that why you're so late?" Now Lizzy's eyes practically sparkled, and my mom was trying hard not to grin.

"Stop it right there, both of you. I barely know her. Well, that's not quite right. I kind of know her even though it's only been three days. But it's only been three days. So just stop thinking whatever it is you're thinking." Now it was my turn to shoot them both looks.

Lizzy sank back into the sofa, with a smug smirk on her face. "No problem, James. I'm just thinking one thought. You never use the word 'different' when you're describing a woman. In fact, all of your girlfriends, and I do mean all, were described the same way. You would say they are pretty, nice, and 'fill in the blank' for whatever their job was. You didn't even say if Ellie was pretty. You didn't say she was nice. And you didn't say what her job is."

With that statement, Lizzy turned to my mom and said "This one *is* different."

Then they both smiled.

And t*hat* was no good for me at all.

Chapter 18

- *Ellie*

I got to cooking class a little bit early. I was embarrassed for myself because I knew I was there early only because I couldn't wait to see James again. It made me feel slightly pathetic. He had been so nice to me over the past couple of days, but I wasn't sure if that was specific to me, or if he was just that kind of guy.

I walked up to my workstation and waved a small hello to Chef Mike and his assistant—another Mike— as they prepared things at the front of the class. James would be bringing in our groceries from our shopping trip, so there really wasn't anything for me to do. After I stashed my bag under my station, I walked to the front of the room and asked if I could be of any help.

"Hey, Dr. Ellie, we'd love your help. We're just stocking up the supplies for the dishes everyone is making tonight. If you could organize all the dry goods into these bins, that would be great." Chef Mike pointed out the bags that needed to be sorted.

"No problem. And please, call me Ellie." I wasn't surprised that Chef Mike knew my name. After two days in the class, I knew everyone by name as well.

"So, Ellie, how do you like the class?" Chef Mike was busy mixing something together and glanced up to see my response.

"The class has been great. Really. I haven't tried any of the recipes on my own, but I feel like I could make them, which is half the battle, I think."

"Yes, confidence is key when it comes to cooking," he said. "You just have to go for it. And don't let mishaps stop you. Just try, try again. But what do you think about the other part of the class?" Chef Mike stopped what he was doing, and looked right at me, waiting.

I stopped sorting. My hands stilled. "The other part?" The sound of confusion filled my question.

"Yeah, the 'Lonely Hearts Club' part. Since we billed this whole thing as a singles event, what do you think? Have you met some people?"

Now I really was embarrassed, and heat rushed to my face. How should I answer this? I want to be fair to Chef Mike—I did feel like this was a really good way to meet people. And, I'd met James. But was I going to say that? Out loud? I barely admitted to myself what I felt for James.

"Well, it's been fun, and I'm definitely learning how to cook. And James has been a big help. Both Shauna and Brett have been great, too. So yeah, I'd say as a way to meet people, it's been a success." There. That told him the truth, without getting specific about James.

"Glad to hear it. I've had some great feedback from people in the past, but I like to hear from all my classes. And I've gotten to know James a bit—you got lucky when you were paired up with him, I think. He seems like a good guy."

"Were you guys just talking about me?" James asked. He walked into the room and placed our groceries on our workstation, then came to the front of the room.

Chef Mike laughed, and I'm sure I blushed. "You could say that. I just asked Ellie how she felt about the class and said I thought you were a good guy. I was just waiting for her response when you walked in."

They both turned and looked at me, and there was a definite sparkle in Chef Mike's eye. That little matchmaker. He might say he's doing this for charity, but I think he really liked matching people up.

James gave a little laugh and shrugged. "So, what do you think, Ellie? Am I a good guy?" He gave me a devilish grin, but at the same time, I was surprised he appeared the slightest bit nervous like he wasn't sure what my response would be. Huh. Who would have thought?

I didn't have any choice but to play along, something I often struggled to do. So I was going to have to channel Jasmine—she was so good at it.

"What are you talking about? You're not a good guy." I put down the chocolate morsels I'd been sorting and walked right up to him with all of the confidence in the world, and threw my arm around his shoulder. "You're the best guy," I said, then gave him a little shake. I wanted him to understand I really meant it.

Both James and Chef Mike burst out laughing, which is what I was going for. I chuckled, and stepped away from James, back to the supplies. By now, the classroom was filling up, and I quickly finished dividing up the goods and made it back to our workstation. Brett and Shauna were at their spot and looked as happy as ever. "Hey, guys. Can you believe this is our last class?" I rested my hip against the cooktop.

"I know, it's been flying by," Shauna responded.

"Yeah," I said. "I've been out of the hospital for so many days now I'm starting to see how the other half lives. And I might like it." I thought about how far away my real life felt. Between the classes, James, and getting ready for EB, I felt like I was living somebody else's life—like it was fake time or something.

"When do you go back?" Brett sat down next to Shauna, and both were sitting on their stools, right up next to each other.

"Yeah, I was wondering that, too," James said.

"Monday. And it'll be here before I know it. Then back to the grind."

James turned away, then back to us. "Then we'll definitely have to get that cooking night we have planned on the books," he said. "I'd hate for this to be the last night we're all together."

"Don't even think you're getting out of that, James," Shauna said. "We're winning tonight, and you and Ellie will be our servants."

I laughed at Shauna. She must be as competitive as me.

"Okay, but I think it's going to be Ellie's schedule we're working around," James said.

I nodded my head. "Yeah, before the night is over we just need to exchange numbers so I can get my on-call schedule to you and we can pick a date." I said this as though making plans outside of work was an everyday occurrence for me when really I couldn't remember the last time I needed to check my schedule in order to make plans with someone else. It felt good, but it also made me nervous. More time with others meant more time revealing the real me—the me most people would not like. But I'd have to deal with that later.

Chef Mike called us all to attention. "All right, everyone, it's our last night of class—let's make the most of it." The class cheered and clapped, and Chef Mike proceeded to give us the instructions for the night.

"Each couple is going to make one entree, and one side, app, or dessert. You will be judged on the presentation of the item as well as how the item tastes. So that means that you have the opportunity to win first or second place. But wait—there's more. Who ever heard of only first and second place? There's always a third place. So you'll all have one more chance."

Chef Mike walked behind one of the prep tables that was covered by a big white sheet. He whipped the sheet off the table. "Ta-da!" He was quite excited, but I'd guess most of us were confused. We were looking at a table of supplies, not unlike the supplies we'd seen for the past couple of days.

"Let me explain. Yesterday, during our icebreaker, you were paired up with someone who suggested a dish based on your personal 'Food that Puts You in the Mood.' At this table are the ingredients and recipe cards for those dishes. Each couple needs to add one of these dishes to the meal they are preparing tonight. That recipe will be judged on how it tastes, as well as how it pairs with your other dishes. Okay? Then let's begin."

I turned to James. "I'll go get our recipe, you get started on the chicken."

I moved to rush past him, and he stopped me with his hand on my arm.

"Wait. I'm the better cook. Maybe I should do it."

"You're definitely the better cook," I said, "but I'm the best in an emergency, and this feels like an emergency. Besides, just because I don't cook doesn't mean I don't know a ton about how to eat. I got this."

James smiled and nodded. "Go to it, then."

I was back to our workstation in a flash.

"What did you get?" James asked. He looked at my small bin.

"It's your mood food. Peaches. It's a recipe for peach and mango salsa. I thought it would be a great cool sauce to serve with the spicy chicken we're making."

James grinned from ear to ear. "I think you're right. Beautiful and good in an emergency. How did I get so lucky?"

He chuckled and reached for the bin in my arms, but to me, it felt like he was reaching for my heart.

Chapter 19

- James

Ellie worked on the peaches and mangos, while I chopped up the fresh herbs for the salsa. She was right. This peach and mango salsa would be a great side to the spicy chicken. I already had the chicken in the oven, so once we finished the salsa, we could get the chocolate lava cake prepped.

Shauna and Brett were hard at work behind us, and it looked like they opted to do both their entree and side dish from one of their own recipes. A salmon dish with... was that orzo? With parmesan? Fish was a risky choice. It was easy to overcook. And I couldn't tell what their mystery recipe was from the things in their bin.

Brett caught me checking out their goods and laughed. "Eyes on your own work, James. Nothing you find out now can help you with your cooking. The countdown has begun."

Shauna laughed and chimed in. "Yeah, the countdown to our delicious first place win—and to you guys hosting us all... night...long."

Ellie shot the two of them a half-hearted smile. Brett and Shauna fist bumped and got back to work.

I took a second before going back to chopping my herbs and then stopped. "Hey, are you ok?" Something was off. Ellie hadn't spoken much since we'd started cooking, which wasn't normal.

Her head shot up. "Yes. Of course. I'm ok. Why?"

"You just seem a little... quiet, since class started. Are you nervous about the competition? It's not a big deal if we don't win. Hosting Brett and Shauna would actually be kind of fun. It won't feel like we lost."

Ellie pursed her lips together, and she shifted her focus back to the mangos. "Yeah, we should talk about that. I'm not sure my schedule is going to allow me to get together with you guys. I've been out of work these past two days, I've got all this stuff I need to get ready for EB and I haven't touched my application for the Tate. That was the whole reason I took time off. I just don't think I'll be able to do it." Ellie looked up from the mangos she tossed into her bowl but she didn't look me in the eye. "Are you done with the herbs?"

I gave my head a little shake. "Um, yeah. Yeah, let me measure them into the bowl." I reached for the bowl and added the cilantro and basil. What just happened? Before class, we were all talking about our night out together like it was a given, and now Ellie didn't think she could make it? What happened? What did I miss?

- Ellie

"I just need to add the lime juice and a little bit of sugar, and we can get started on the cake." I took the bowl from James, and turned back to my ingredients, trying hard not to see the hurt that flashed across his face. But suddenly I didn't want this. I enjoyed spending time with him, but this was fake time. I didn't have these kinds of breaks in my life, especially with EB and the Tate. If I kept putting that off, Dr. Marks would win for sure, and I couldn't have that. James was a distraction.

Besides, beautiful and good in an emergency? What on earth? He barely knew me, and I needed to keep it that way. I always kept it that way. It was better for everyone. Other than Jasmine, no one knew me beyond the surface. He might think my looks were beautiful, and of course, I was good in an emergency, but that was all stuff you could see. That was all the public me. The me I'd worked hard to show the world. If he knew more about me, if he knew about the things I'd done, and more importantly, what I hadn't done...he wouldn't think that at all.

I needed to stop this little infatuation thing I had going on with him. I didn't want what he wanted in life. I would never want those things. There was a reason I kept my dating to just dates. I don't fall for the guy, and I wasn't going to start now. He already knew more about me than I wanted, so I needed to just stop before it got any more out of hand.

I finished mixing up the salsa and set the bowl over to the side. James got the double boiler and was busy pulling out the ingredients we would need. I was glad he was busy, so I wouldn't have to look him in—

James stood straight up from getting out the last of the ingredients and turned directly to me. "I understand the words 'you don't have time,' but I thought you wanted to get together with Brett and Shauna."

He spoke in a pretty low voice, but something in the way he stood or talked made both Shauna and Brett lift their heads from where they worked on the orzo. They glanced back and forth to each other and back to us, and then put their heads down. *Swell. An audience.*

I took a deep breath. I had to put a stop to this. "I did. I do. I just... really, I just don't have time." I was biting my lip at this point and tried to say the least possible. If I kept talking, I would say something that I didn't want to.

James looked at me. "I thought you wanted to get together..." He paused. "With me."

I didn't know how someone so handsome, smart, and kind could sound so unsure of himself, but somehow I'd made it happen.

Now I was biting my lip hard. What was I doing? I did want to get together with him. I really did. I just... couldn't.

"I'm sorry." That's all I could say.

James turned and reached for the chocolate. "No problem, Dr. Ellie. I get it."

Doctor. Ellie.

Whatever we had, I knew it had just ended.

And I wondered if the sick feeling that hit my stomach would ever go away.

Class was taking forever. Yet Shauna and Brett were having a great time. Heck, everyone seemed to be having a great time. Just not James and me. I mean, James continued to be cordial—of course he would continue to be nice. But it was obvious I'd disappointed him, and I couldn't seem to find a way out of it. Even when I sliced up a couple of strawberries into a pretty fan shape—one of the assistants helped me with that—to put on the plate with the chocolate lava cake, I only got a small smile and "I think Chef Mike will like that," before he turned back to making the whipped cream.

The judging for the contest started at the front of the classroom, and Chef Mike and one of his assistants slowly made their way around the room. There was a lot of laughter. Chef Mike nailed it with his cooking class.

By the time James added the whipped cream and a little drizzle of chocolate sauce to the cake, Chef Mike was with Shauna and Brett, and James and I were both eavesdropping.

"I love the pairing of your creamy orzo with the sweet and spicy salmon. It's a delicious combination, and the textures are great together. And this salmon is cooked perfectly. What method did you use to cook it?" Chef Mike took a bite of the salmon as though he hadn't already tasted three entrees tonight.

Shauna gave him a big grin. "I play cooking shows at home for background noise. One day I saw a show that said the best way to cook salmon was 'low and slow' in the oven. We knew we'd have a lot of time tonight, so that's what we did."

Chef Mike took one more bite, scooping up both the salmon and orzo onto his fork. He closed his eyes and moaned in appreciation. "You guys did good. Well done." He clapped Brett on the shoulder and winked at Shauna. Shauna squealed and jumped at Brett, who caught her in a big hug. I shot James a look, but he was already greeting Chef Mike.

"Ok, let's see what you guys have got. You went with your own entree, right?"

James nodded and answered. "We did. Dr. Ellie wanted to learn some more recipes, so we did a spicy chicken thigh bake with the lava cake for dessert."

Chef Mike nodded along and pointed to the salsa. "And the peach and mango salsa?"

James waited for me, so I replied. "I thought a cool salsa would work well with the spicy chicken dish, but I wasn't expecting the recipe to call for jalapenos. After James and I talked about it, I just took the spicy elements out, so we got the cooling effect we wanted."

"Great idea. Alright, let me get a taste." Chef Mike reached for the plate, gave it a once-over, and took a bite. "Very nice, you guys. The chicken thigh is tender with just a bit of spice, and the salsa pairs with it nicely. Good job taking the heat out of the salsa." He took another bite. "My wife and I have an affinity for mango salsa, but I've never added the peaches. Nice touch."

James grinned at me like a proud parent, which made me laugh in spite of myself. I liked him. I did. He just wouldn't like me if he knew the real me, so what was the point?

"Alright, now for your dessert. Which is the third lava cake I've tasted tonight. I think it's a hit. I'll have to be sure to use that recipe again in future classes." He picked up the lava cake. "I like the little strawberry flourish you did here. Strawberries and chocolate are a classic pairing. I'm happy to see it." Chef Mike dug in, and we got the same closed-eye response that Brett and Shauna got for the salmon. "Really good, you guys. You did good work here." He shot us a quick grin and moved to the table in front of us.

I turned to James, and now I was the one who squealed like Shauna did minutes ago. But there was no way I was going to throw myself into James's arms.

No matter how much I wanted to.

Chapter 20

- James

I hated this. Everything in me said I should be hugging Ellie right now, but based on what was said earlier, there was no way that would be something she would want. I had to make myself busy, or my arms were going to go around her regardless of what my brain told me.

I picked up the plate of chocolate lava cake that Chef Mike didn't eat, and handed it to Ellie. "Congratulations. I think he liked what we did," I said, and then reached for the piece that had a bite out of it. I didn't mind—I'd shared with my sister and brothers all my life.

"Thanks, James. I think so, too." Ellie gave me a big smile and dug into the cake.

Shauna and Brett were both on their stools, eating... "Is that banana pudding?" I asked, and pulled my stool closer to their station.

"Yeah, this was our mystery recipe. It's really good, too. A southern recipe if I've ever made one. Have some if you want." Shauna pushed the bowl towards my side of the table.

"So, what do you guys think? Chef Mike is about to wrap up at the last table. Who is he going to go with as the winner?"

Brett was grinning from ear to ear, and so was Shauna. Obviously, they both thought they were going to win.

Ellie pulled up her stool. "I think it's going to be close. He did seem to like your meal, but he liked what we did too. Right, James?" Ellie's competitive side was cute, and I liked that about her. Of course, I liked a lot of things about her, except for whatever it was that put her off earlier in the class.

I gave her a warm smile. "Yeah, I think it's going to be close."

Right then Chef Mike called for our attention. "Ok, everyone, I have our winners. But first, I want to thank you guys for being here and for being such great students over the past couple of days. A handful of you really weren't cooks at all, and I hope you are feeling much more confident about your abilities now. Give yourselves a round of applause."

The class clapped and some people yelled out how awesome Chef Mike was.

"Thank you, guys, thank you. It's been a lot of fun. Now let's get to the winners."

There was more applause, and Chef Mike called out, "Everyone did great. This was a fun class to judge. First—honorable mention—which I wasn't even planning on doing—goes out to...James and Ellie."

There was a round of cheering and Ellie and I just looked at each other, disappointment on Ellie's face. I shrugged, and I didn't hold back. I put my arm around her shoulder. "Maybe next time," I said, then let her go.

Like there was going to be a next time.

Chef Mike was still talking. "They did a great job of adapting the mystery recipe to go with their meal. And their chocolate lava cake not only tasted great but looked great in its presentation. Okay, on to third place."

Shauna leaned over her workstation and said, "Good for you guys. But you've got to know we're sitting back here hoping we're going to win it. Free dinner on the line." She flashed us crossed fingers, and we both laughed.

"For third place, for best integration of the mystery recipe into their meal, is Jamal and Nira. They added a roasted eggplant sauce to their pork tenderloin. It was a great combination of flavors and highlighted the pork. It was also not something you see together every day, and I liked their originality."

Everyone clapped, Jamal and Nira hugged and laughed, and Ellie watched them the whole time, a contemplative expression on her face. I wondered what, exactly, she was thinking.

"For second place, for best tasting side dish, it's... Brett and Shauna." Shauna jumped off her stool and practically landed in Brett's lap, laughing the whole time. And before she could get a word out, Chef Mike said. "And first place...Brett and Shauna, for the best tasting entree."

There was a lot of good-natured cheering with some groans thrown out by the people who hadn't won anything, and Brett lifted Shauna off his lap, stood up, and spun her around. They were both laughing, and he leaned in and kissed her, mid-spin.

The class went wild over the kiss, and Chef Mike said, "I think we can definitely say at least two people are no longer part of the *Lonely Hearts Club*!"

Brett placed Shauna back on her feet and grabbed her hand, then the two of them, both still laughing, took a bow for the whole class.

I went around the workstation and hugged Shauna and clapped Brett on the back. "You did it. You won. Looks like we'll be treating you to a home-cooked dinner at my place." I glanced over to Ellie as I said it. She didn't have to follow through with the plans if she didn't want to, but I wasn't going to be the one to tell them about her backing out.

Ellie smiled at Brett and Shauna, but she didn't walk around the tabletop. She stayed on her side. "Congratulations, you guys—that was awesome. And yeah, I'm just going to have to check my schedule, like I said earlier." She looked between the three of us, not settling her gaze. She was uncomfortable.

Chef Mike called us all to attention and wrapped up the class. "Thank you guys again for being such good students. I know the charities that this benefited are grateful, and I hope you all benefitted as well. Both on the food and friendship front. Be sure to drop in to eat and say hello sometime, and never forget—if you can't be incredible, at least your meals can be!"

The class cheered and applauded, and yelled out thanks to Chef Mike. Class was ending on a high note. Well, for almost everyone.

One of the guys from the front of the room yelled out. "For anyone who wants to, we're going to continue the evening at the restaurant bar. Chef Mike is going to stop by so we can buy him a drink. Hope to see you all there."

I made my way back to my workstation, where Ellie pulled out her purse. I pushed my stool up to the station. Brett and Shauna had grabbed their things and were moving toward us.

"You guys going to the bar? We have to go and buy Chef Mike a drink. I mean, we have to. Being the winners and all." Brett laughed before he even finished his sentence.

"Yeah, yeah, we know, big winners," I said. "I'm going."

"Ellie?" Shauna asked.

"I can't. I have so much work to catch up on and only one day to do it. Sorry, guys."

I wasn't surprised by her response at all.

"Aw, really, Ellie? Not even for one drink? We'd really like you there." Shauna reached out and put her hand on Ellie's arm. "Come on. It's fun."

"Thanks, you guys, but I can't," she replied.

I had my hands stuffed in my front jeans pockets, and let this conversation take place without my input. Ellie was going to have to let them down on her own.

"Well, okay, but we have to get your number before we go. We've got to get that home-cooked meal you owe us on the calendar." Shauna pulled out her phone and handed it to Ellie, then we all exchanged numbers.

"I'll text you soon with my schedule," Ellie said.

We all moved toward the exit of the classroom, while I thought about how Ellie was going to back out of our deal by text, and not face to face. Seemed a bit cowardly on her part, since she already told me her intentions. Shauna and Brett moved through the doors toward the front of the restaurant, when Ellie surprised me by placing her hand on my arm.

"James. I wanted to thank you."

She stopped walking, so I did too.

"For?" I asked.

"Everything. For being such a great cooking partner. For being so easy to get along with. But especially, for everything you helped me with today. I couldn't have gotten ready for EB without you. So thank you."

Her hand was still on my arm, and because I was a nice guy, I patted it. "You're welcome, Ellie. Good luck with everything." And I turned and walked away.

Just like she wanted me to.

Chapter 21

- Ellie

I walked away with my back straight and my head high, but my legs felt weak, as though they knew—independent of the rest of my body—that I didn't want to leave James.

Brett and Shauna called out "goodbye" from the bar, where they sat on tall stools, facing each other, and so close together that their legs were intertwined. I was jealous of how easily they had fallen into what looked like a legitimate relationship. I wanted that. But couldn't have it. Especially with James. I liked him too much to do that to him.

James stood next to Brett with his back against the bar, and he gave me a little two-finger salute. I gave a small wave back to the three of them, a general wave to the rest of the class, and walked out of the restaurant.

I realized then that Chef Mike hadn't joined the others at the bar yet, and I hadn't said thank you and goodbye. I stopped walking. Should I go back in? It was a perfect excuse. And for all of my not wanting to pursue something with James, I also really wanted to pursue something with James. I hated this feeling.

I kept walking, knowing that the smartest thing I could do was go home, try to get a little work done that I desperately needed to do, and prepare for another day of getting ready for EB.

- James

The bar was loud and I was bummed.

Ellie had walked out with barely a goodbye, and though that wasn't a surprise, deep down I wanted her to change her mind.

"Shots! Shots! Shots!" Jamal called out, and the next thing I knew shots were lined up in front of everyone from the class. Chef Mike joined us, and Jamal explained that he had just ordered shots of 'Sex on the Beach' for everyone to celebrate the class. Apparently, the theme of 'Food that Gets You in the Mood' was continuing into the bar.

Brett and Shauna were as excited as anyone and joined in with the "shots, shots, shots" chant. I was happy for them, but I wasn't in the mood. I decided to do one shot, stick around long enough to drink a glass of water, and then call it a night.

"Everyone have their shot?" Jamal looked over the group and made sure everyone had their drink. He raised his up and we all followed suit. "To Chef Mike. The best chef, the best teacher, and the best matchmaker around. Hear, hear!"

A chorus of "hear, hear" and "cheers" went up, and there was a second of silence from our group while everyone drank. The noise of a multitude of shot glasses landing back on the bar top rang out, and then everyone was back to laughter and conversation.

I asked the bartender for a glass of water when Brett ordered two beers. "You want one, James? It's the least I can do, knowing you and Ellie will be serving us dinner soon."

I shook my head and declined. "Nah, I'm just going to drink this water, and head out. I'm not feeling it tonight."

Shauna gave me a sympathetic smile. "I was really hoping Ellie was going to join us tonight. I like her and wanted to get to know her better."

"Yeah, me too. But I wasn't surprised when she turned down our invitation. She said she's really busy with work."

"Yeah, that's too bad," Brett added. "But that's okay, we'll get to know her better when we get together again."

I took a big gulp of water and wondered how to say this. "I don't think that's going to happen. She told me earlier tonight that with work and some personal things going on she didn't think she was going to make it to our cookout."

Shauna sat up straight with a shocked look on her face. "What? Why? She can't do that. I didn't hear her say that."

"She said it to me. Earlier tonight. I guess she didn't want to disappoint you guys, so she didn't say anything at the end of class."

Shauna was insistent. "But she said she'd get her schedule to us. Surely she's not going to back out. We've been having so much fun."

I finished my water and set it on the counter. "I know. I thought the same thing. So listen, I'm going to head out. But no matter what, the three of us will get together, even if Ellie doesn't join us. It'll be her loss if she doesn't."

I gave them a smile, but I bet they could both tell it wasn't a real one. Shauna jumped off her stool and gave me a hug. "Okay, James. Have a good night, and we'll make plans soon. I know I'm not ready for this to all end." She turned her gaze to Brett with that sentence, and he was looking right at her.

Brett clapped me on the shoulder. "Alright, man. Be safe driving home. And we'll make plans soon, okay?" Brett stepped back to Shauna and put his arm around her shoulders.

"Yep. Sounds good. See you guys."

I said goodbye to a couple more classmates, and let Chef Mike know I'd be back soon to enjoy a meal at his restaurant, then headed for the doors. I stepped out onto the sidewalk when I got a text. I was sure it would be Lizzy. We had made tentative plans for me to see baby James tomorrow at some point.

I reached for my cell phone and walked to my truck. I stopped cold. The text wasn't from my sister—it was from Ellie. With the most unexpected words I could have imagined.

Dr. Ellie: *James. It's Ellie. Can you call me when you leave the bar? I need you.*

Chapter 22

- Ellie

I paced my apartment. I'd just texted James, still holding the phone in my hand, and now I wished I could take it back. *Shoot, shoot, shoot.* Barely any time had passed since I treated him so poorly and walked out of that class, and now I was texting him. He was going to think I was crazy.

And I was. A little crazy. I couldn't get closer to him, but at the same time, the thought of maybe never seeing him again...I couldn't stomach it.

Besides, I did need him. I did.

Ugh. Need. I hated needing anyone for anything. Though if I were being honest with myself, this kind of need felt different. My heart rate was up, and a slight sweat broke out on my hairline. It definitely wasn't because of the pacing.

If James really knew me, if he knew about what I'd done in the past—or more accurately, what I'd failed to do in my past—he wouldn't want anything to do with me. Especially considering how much he loved children and wanted them in his future.

Being a temporary caregiver to EB was the closest I would ever get to being a parent. That's it. And that was temporary. I purposely went into the specialized field of infertility because I loved children and knew I would never have any. I was so happy for all of the parents I helped who were struggling. Those parents wanted to have children. It wasn't an accident, it wasn't a mistake, they were fighting for it, and they were fighting for those kids. That child was the most important thing to them, and I was so lucky that I could help.

But that was it. That was as close as I got.

Until now.

With EB.

I paced back and forth. This was such a bad idea. Why had I texted him? He might be mad at me. He might be having such a good time at the bar he didn't see the text for hours.

Pausing at the window I looked out at the street, but that did no good—I couldn't stand still. Maybe James wasn't mad at me, but maybe he just wouldn't want to talk to me after the way I'd left things.

The phone I was still holding in my hand rang, and jerked me out of my thoughts.

I hit the green 'accept' button. "James?"

James's voice rushed through the phone. "Ellie. Hi, yeah. Is everything okay?"

Shoot. He sounded a bit panicked. I didn't mean to panic him.

"Yes, yes, everything is fine. I'm sorry, I didn't mean to scare you, I just needed to ask you for another favor."

He whooshed out a breath. "Oh. Okay. After the night we had, the last thing I expected was to get a text. I thought something was wrong."

Ouch. Of course he didn't expect a text from me. I basically acted like I never wanted to see him again. In the short amount of time I'd spent with James, I should've known he would say exactly what was on his mind. Like in class earlier, when he said he thought I wanted to hang out not only with Shauna and Brett but with him, too. He was definitely straightforward.

"No, not wrong, exactly. But I need your help. The furniture store is open tomorrow, but they don't do same-day delivery on Sundays. Tomorrow is the only day I have to get the other furniture pieces I need for EB's room, and the only day I have to get it to my apartment before the home inspection. And I know you have a truck. So I need you."

This time I got a slight chuckle before I heard his sigh. But it wasn't exactly an 'I think you're funny' chuckle, it was more like an 'I think you're exasperating' chuckle. This call was going about as good as I thought it would after I'd hit 'send' on my text. Not good at all.

"So you don't need *me*, exactly. More like you need my truck."

Again with the ouch. But he wasn't wrong. Exactly.

"You're right. I do need your truck. But I know other people with trucks. I wanted to ask...you."

Now I was pacing again. I bit my lip, bit my tongue, waiting to see what he'd say about that.

What was I doing? Didn't I just say I couldn't get closer to him? And yet...I couldn't help myself. The thought of my life going back to exactly the way it was, without James in it...I didn't like that thought at all. So here I was. Waiting.

There was a pause. A significant pause. But at least there wasn't a sigh this time.

"Okay, Ellie. I have plans with my sister tomorrow, which I don't want to change, since Sunday is pretty much my only day off. But I'm sure I can meet you at the furniture store later in the afternoon. What time does the store close?"

This time it was me who sighed, in relief. "It closes at six. And I can pick out everything online tonight, so we just have to be there in time for closing. And thank you, James. I really appreciate it."

"No problem. And you know what? How about I just pick you up at 5:30, and we'll go over together. No need to have two cars there."

"Perfect. That sounds perfect."

And it was.

"Ok. See you tomorrow, Ellie."

"Thanks, James. Bye."

"Bye."

I stopped pacing, I took a big breath, and I smiled.

I was going to see James tomorrow.

- James

I stood on the sidewalk outside the restaurant and shook my head.

That girl.

She had me twisted up. Would she really have called me if she had other friends with a truck? Did she decide she wanted to hang out with me? A million thoughts ran through my head, and I had no way to get the answers to any of them. At least not until I saw her and could talk to her again.

I walked to my truck and got in and decided to call my sister. I texted her first, in case the baby was asleep. My phone rang immediately.

"Hey, sis.' I said, picking up. "How's the little guy? Not asleep, I take it?" I put the phone on hands-free and started up my truck.

"Nope, he is bright-eyed and bushy-tailed. I'm just walking around with him. What are you up to? Just finishing your cooking class? Oh, hey, how was cool Ellie?" Lizzy asked, and I could hear her footsteps in the background.

Dang it. I was going to have to tell her about Ellie. I pulled out of my parking spot and headed for home. Home was about twenty minutes out of the city, and it was exactly where I wanted to be right now.

"Speaking of..." I said. "Turns out you know Ellie."

Her footsteps stopped. "I know Ellie?"

"You do. She's the doc that delivered baby James."

There was a long pause. So long in fact....

"Lizzy? You still there?"

"I am." I heard her walking again. "I just...I'm...huh. I've got nothin'."

I chuckled. "Well, there's a first time for everything. But I know you'll think of something. In the meantime, what time is good for me to come over tomorrow?"

"Baby James usually wakes up early and then takes a morning nap. How about 11 or so? He should be up, and you know Mom and Dad will be making brunch."

"Yep, one of the reasons Sunday is my favorite day. Do you know if dad got blueberries?" My mouth watered, while I thought of his famous blueberry pancakes. He individually placed each blueberry, so the batter didn't turn color. And there were more blueberries than pancake, which is why they were perfect.

Lizzy scoffed. "You know he did. I don't think there has ever been a brunch without his blueberry pancakes."

"What about the boys? Any of them going to make it?" You never knew with my brothers.

"Not this week. But Mom has come up with some 'newfangled' breakfast cocktail—her words. So be prepared to be a guinea pig. It can't be me. Breastfeeding."

I groaned. "I already know more about breastfeeding than I ever thought I'd need to know. I thought I'd have my own before I knew so much."

Lizzy laughed at me. "No time like the present to learn. Besides, I think you're behind on your lifetime plan. You've always wanted kids. You know, kids like the good doctor delivers. I never thought I'd have one before you."

Working in another comment about Ellie didn't take her long.

And she did make me pause. I wasn't exactly old, but I was 35. That didn't leave a ton of years ahead of me. When had growing my business taken precedence over growing a family?

"Yeah," I replied. "I didn't see it happening this way either. I really thought that Leesl was the one. Well, Leesl or Cathy. Or Susan. Susan was good."

Lizzy burst out laughing on the other end of the line. "Do you hear your big uncle talking? Do you?" I guess she was talking to the baby now. "He is just a crazy man. So crazy. Just listen to him. 'Leesl. Or Cathy. Or Susan.' He is so funny. Such a funny uncle you have."

I cut in. "You know I can hear you, right?"

Lizzy still laughed. "Yeah, I know you can hear me. But did you hear me? 'Cause that is all you. Just listen to yourself. Who has three women—three—that they think was the one? I bet if you thought about it, you would come up with at least two more. Heck, I can come up with two more. What about Beth and Diane? Or Linda? That's three more! Weren't they also, 'the one?'"

She had a point. But it wasn't a point I wanted to think about. "Ok, now you're just making me mad."

"I'm not trying to make you mad, James. I'm trying to point out you've had a lot of girlfriends over the years that could all be the one. And yet, not one of them was. Maybe you should think about that."

"How did we end up talking about me, when I just wanted to solidify plans for pancakes?" I grumbled, pulling up to my house.

"Think about it, big brother. Just think about it. Now I'm going to see if I can breastfeed this baby, and put him to bed. I'll see you tomorrow Uncle James."

She hung up before I could reply.

And she was wrong. Those past girlfriends of mine, each one could have been the one. They just…weren't. That wasn't my fault…was it?

Chapter 23

- *Ellie*

James would be here to pick me up at any minute, and I was ready. Once again I'd broken out of my standard home uniform of scrubs and spent a little bit more time getting ready. I wore my favorite jeans, a lightweight ivory cashmere sweater that I never seemed to find an opportunity to wear, and Converse tennis shoes. My hair was up in its typical messy bun—we did have work to do after all—but I put on more makeup than I normally would on a weekend home alone. Specifically *because* I wouldn't be home alone. I'd be with James.

I'd placed the order with the furniture store, and it was ready to be picked up. I also placed a big order with Target for a bunch of things that I thought EB might need. I remembered my time in foster care and also referred to the info the Child Protective Services caseworker, Mrs. Gonzalez, shared with me. Mrs. Gonzalez was great, like most of the caseworkers I knew growing up. It was the judges and lawyers you had to be careful of.

I ordered some toiletries, bedding for her bedroom, and a little bit of clothing, including pajamas. I wanted her to pick out her own clothes if she wanted to.

I even had plans to surprise James with dinner, as a thank you. I wanted to make up for how I'd treated him at the cooking class. I googled 'easy chicken and vegetable dinner' and settled on a stir fry that didn't look too hard. Chinese takeout was one of my favorite things, and I liked the thought of being able to make it myself.

I ordered the groceries online and picked them up earlier in the day. It had taken much longer than I thought it would to prep the meat and vegetables. I hadn't given much thought to how much easier it was to cook with another person like I'd done with James in cooking class, but everything was ready now and shouldn't take too long to make once James was here. I was making a big assumption that James would stay.

I hoped he would stay.

I was all over the place when it came to him.

And if it was making me crazy, I wondered what it was doing to him?

I'd asked James to text me when he arrived, so he wouldn't have to find a parking spot. I wanted to make this as easy on him as possible. I decided to make my way outside to wait for him when I got his text.

James: *I'm out front.*
Me: Be right there!

My stomach erupted with nerves. I grabbed my purse, and dashed out the door, locking it behind me. I had a lot of making up to do, and I wasn't sure how he was going to take it.

- James

I hated that I felt nervous. This was Ellie. Ellie, the girl who had made it clear that she didn't want anything to do with me, but she did need a truck. So I guess there was that.

I barely had a chance to breathe before she pulled open the passenger door, and climbed in. She looked so good. And smelled so good. Of course she did.

"Hey, James. Thanks. Thanks so much for picking me up."

"Right. No problem. I've already got the store plugged into the GPS. Is there anything else you need?"

Shoot, I didn't mean to sound cold, but that came out a bit rougher than I expected it to. She heard it in my voice, too.

She sat up straight. "Nope. Just the store. And then back here to carry everything in. That's it." She gazed out the window, and I already hated this.

"Ellie. Sorry about that, I didn't mean to be so short. I just meant, are we good to go?"

She turned her head to me, and I could tell she was trying to decide which way to go with this.

She inhaled deeply. Decision made, apparently. "That's okay. I really do appreciate what you're doing for me, and I'd like to make it up to you."

"You do?" I asked. "How?" I was caught off guard and it showed.

She laughed out loud. "Surprised you, did I?"

"Yes, yes you did." I put the truck in drive and pulled onto the road. "Exactly how were you planning on making it up to me?" I had a whole host of ideas that she could try, but based on everything she had said the night before, none of those seemed likely to happen. Ever.

"I'd like to make you dinner tonight as a thank you," she said.

I flashed her a quick glance and went to answer when she interrupted me.

"I know, I know, I'm just learning to cook. But you and Chef Mike were both really good teachers, and I think I can pull this off. Besides, you'll be there, if anything looks like it is going off track."

"So what you are saying is *I* am making us dinner tonight?" I gave her a smirk, and she laughed. She reached out and gently pushed my shoulder.

So she was touching me. Interesting. Maybe this night wasn't going to go as I thought.

"No, no. Not at all. I already bought and prepped everything, it just needs to be cooked. And I think that should be pretty easy. Do you like chicken and vegetable stir fry?"

I glanced over, and she bit her lip, waiting for my response.

Oh, I could make this so hard on her. But that didn't feel right at all. So I answered honestly.

"I do like chicken stir fry. It's one of my favorites, in fact. And thank you. I would love to have you make me dinner." I looked over and gave her a half smile, then pulled into the furniture store parking lot.

Ellie pointed out the window. "Right over there, where it says 'customer pick-up'. I'll jump out and let them know we're here."

I pulled over to the side, and Ellie got out of the car. "Back in a minute," she said and slammed the door shut.

I needed a second before she got back to the car. I needed to reassess the evening. I didn't want to guess what was going on with her—why she went from 'sorry, no time for you,' to 'please stay for dinner.' When we got to her place, I would ask her what was up. In the meantime, she was making an effort, so I would too. I hoped this girl wasn't playing me for a fool.

It wasn't long before Ellie and an employee came out of the store, rolling the dresser and nightstand out on a small hand dolly. I got out of the truck to help the guy get them into the back.

"I asked if we could borrow the hand cart for the night since we're the last people picking up. I can drop it back here in the morning." Ellie moved out of the way.

"Excellent. That'll be easier than the two of us dragging these things in."

I turned to the employee and shook his hand. "Thanks for your help, we'll take it from here."

Ellie and I got back into the truck and headed to her place.

"Thanks again for doing this. I feel like I'm really moving forward with this whole EB thing," she said.

And I hoped we were moving forward with the whole James and Ellie thing, too.

Chapter 24

- Ellie

James unboxed and put together the two pieces of furniture, while I worked on the stir fry. At one point he exclaimed so loudly, I had to run into the other room and make sure I didn't need my first aid kit. I had to admit, there was a tiny part of me that wanted to impress him with my suturing skills, but he was just frustrated with trying to get the drawers together. Turns out prefab furniture could even best a master builder. Who knew?

I promised to call him if anything seemed like it was about to go downhill with my meal. I was a bit late getting the rice on the stove, but I could still make it work. I wanted this to be perfect. Not perfect the way I always wanted things to be a certain way, but perfect for him. He deserved that.

I was so glad he took me up on my offer of dinner, especially after the way I'd left class the night before. I hoped that when we sat down to eat, he would be his straightforward self, because I wanted to tell him. I desperately wanted to tell him how I felt about him, and why I was giving off such confusing signals. I wanted to. But could I?

"I've got the dresser and nightstand set up, and the boxes broken down. How are things going in here?" James walked into the kitchen.

"Good, I think we're both going to be happy with this—or at least I hope so." I shot him a smile over my shoulder, then turned back to the stove. I loved having him here. With me. In my kitchen. Together.

"Anything I can do to help?" James stepped closer to the island but didn't come closer to me.

I wanted him to come closer to me.

"Um, yeah. How about you grab us plates and silverware, and some water from the fridge. I'll just finish this up and get it on the table."

When he didn't move closer to me, my big idea to tell him how I felt didn't seem like the best idea I ever had. It seemed more like I was setting myself up for a big rejection. Really big. I could feel the panic starting to rise.

But wait. I could do this. This was James. If he was going to let me down, at least he would let me down easy.

I grabbed two bowls, put the stir-fry in one and the rice in the other, and then brought them to the table. James had the table set, and I got serving spoons and napkins, and we both took a seat.

"Wow, Ellie. This looks good," James looked over the dishes while a smile slowly slid onto his face.

I held up my hands in front of me and crossed my fingers.

"Fingers crossed," I said. "Let's try it and find out." I pushed the rice closer to James. We both filled up our plates, and James raised his eyebrows.

I held my breath.

"Ok, let's do this. On three," James said. "One, two, three." We both took a bite.

I tasted my bite, and my head shot up. "Not bad, right?" I could feel my shoulders start to relax and the knot in my stomach untie.

James held up one finger and took another bite. With a perfectly straight face, he looked me right in the eye. "Ellie. I think you've done it. You have prepared a meal, not only one that did not involve peanut butter or jelly, but also one that involved pots and pans. But most importantly of all, it tastes delicious." He placed his hand over his heart. "I could not be more proud."

By the time he finished talking, he was smiling from ear to ear, and it matched mine. It was crazy how good that felt, hearing those words coming from him. Now *I* couldn't be more proud.

I lifted my hand above the table for a fist bump. "Look at me. I did it." I could barely contain myself.

James tipped his chin, and his knuckles met mine.

I raised my eyebrows. "Okay, then, let's eat!"

James laughed at my enthusiasm, and we were both quiet for a moment, digging into dinner. I decided to capitalize on the good feeling I was riding, and go ahead and spill my guts.

I set my fork down and reached for my water, then cleared my throat. James's eyes were instantly on mine.

"I wanted to apologize for the way I acted yesterday in class."

James sat back in his chair. "Yeah? In what way do you mean?" He set his fork down.

Okay, so I was doing this. I took a big breath.

"Well, I went from making informal plans with you, Shauna, and Brett, and then the next thing I did was make it clear I wouldn't have time for any of that." I paused and took another breath. "That I wouldn't have time for you."

There. I said it. Now, he just needed to...

"Why did you do that?"

Shoot. That's not what I wanted him to say. I wanted him to say "thanks, no problem, don't worry about it" but of course, he didn't say that. James didn't beat around the bush. And truthfully, I liked that about him. I didn't have to guess where things stood. The least I could do was be as straightforward as him.

"Well..." Was I really going to tell him? I paused. "It's not because I didn't want to spend more time with you," I said. "Because I did. I do."

He waited for me to go on.

"You know how I told you I grew up in foster care?" He nodded slowly and didn't take his eyes off me.

I reached for another drink of water, then let my hand fall. I wanted to tell him everything. Like, everything. But I needed a little liquid courage if I was going to keep that knot in my stomach at bay. "Hey, would you like a beer? Or a glass of wine? I'm going to have a glass of wine." Before I could stand up, he reached across the table and put his hand over mine.

"You don't ha—"

The buzzer for my apartment went off and I grabbed the opportunity to buy some time. I leaped up from my chair and dashed to the door. "That's Target making a delivery. I ordered a bunch of stuff for EB. Let me just buzz them up," I called out as I left the room.

I pressed the intercom, and said, "Come on up. I'm here," and then buzzed the street door open.

James was eating again when I made it back to the kitchen. I went to the refrigerator to pull out a bottle of white wine. "Anything for you?" I asked, and he shook his head no. I placed it on the counter and reached for a glass when there was a knock on the door.

"Coming," I called out.

I opened up the door and was completely taken aback when Jasmine walked in, Chinese takeout in her hands.

"I figured there was no way you would want to cook after all of your cooking classes," she said. "And there was no way I could wait 'til Monday to hear about all your 'fun,' as you described it, so I picked up—"

Jasmine stopped in her tracks. "Oh. I'm sorry. I'm Jasmine," she said.

She took a step back and turned to look at me. "And who is this?"

She turned her head from me to James and back to me, with both confusion and delight crossing her face.

Shoot. Jasmine. I hadn't told her a thing.

This wasn't going to go well.

Not at all.

Chapter 25

- James

I pushed back my chair, glanced at Ellie, stood up from the table, and walked over to Jasmine. "Here, let me get that for you." I reached for the takeout bags and set them down on the island, then turned back and held out my hand. "Hi, I'm James. I'm a friend of Ellie's," I said, shaking Jasmine's hand.

"You're a friend of Ellie's?" She put a slight emphasis on Ellie's name. She glanced at Ellie, and back to me. "I thought I knew all of Ellie's friends." The way she said it, I think she *did* know all of Ellie's friends.

"Um, he's a friend from my cooking class." Ellie moved towards us from the door, where she had seemingly been frozen.

"From cooking class?" It was supposed to be a question, but it was more of a statement. "The Sgt. Pepper's Lonely Hearts Club Cooking Class? The one that was set up as a singles event? The same cooking class that just ended yesterday? And you're here tonight?"

Jasmine rattled off these questions rapid-fire, looking between both Ellie and me, with her eyes and face lit up like she couldn't wait to hear the response.

I couldn't wait for the answer, either, so I turned to Ellie, too.

"Well, yes." Ellie kind of stuttered her response out. "I wanted to thank him." I could tell she was still a little shocked that it was Jasmine who arrived, and not Target. "Why are you here?"

Jasmine gave her a playful grin. "Like I said. I didn't think you'd want to cook, and I didn't want to wait 'til tomorrow to hear about the weekend. I knew if I texted you would say you were too busy working on your research to be interrupted. And I'm super glad I interrupted. You're a completely different kind of busy."

Jasmine was in the kitchen grabbing a plate and fork like she had done this many times before. "I think I should try yours." She looked at Ellie. "Can I try yours? I know what I picked up is good. But how is yours?" Her energy filled the room.

"It's good, and there's plenty," I said and scooted my chair over so she could sit down. "Ellie came far, in just a couple of days."

Jasmine chuckled. "I bet she did," she said, under her breath, and took a bite of the stir fry.

Her gaze shot to Ellie, shock and delight written across her expressive face. "This is... good. Like really good. Like, no one would ever believe that before this you've been known to ruin Ramen. And that's virtually impossible." She took another bite, and Ellie sat down, shoving Jasmine good-naturedly in the shoulder as she moved past. I sat down too, and we all continued to eat.

"So what are you thanking him for?" Jasmine scooped a bit more rice onto her plate.

"What?" Ellie said.

"You said you wanted to thank James. What did he do that you needed to thank him?" She looked right at me then and gave me a big smile. So I answered.

"For helping her build the bunk beds. And for picking up the extra furniture she needed."

Jasmine's head came up from her meal, her eyebrows pulled together. "You're changing your office into a guest bedroom? With bunk beds? What on earth do you need bunk beds for?" She took another bite of dinner.

I answered before Ellie did. "For her niece. EB."

Jasmine's eyebrows pulled in tight, and she set her fork down on her plate. "Ellie doesn't have a niece. She doesn't have any fam...." Once again, shock crossed her face. She turned fully to Ellie.

"You have a niece? EB?" she asked, and like earlier, this wasn't a question. Any playfulness was gone, too.

Ellie took a big breath. "I do."

I wasn't sure what was going on at this moment, but Jasmine's face had dropped.

"Who I know nothing about?" Jasmine said.

"Jasmine, I was going to—" Ellie started to say, but Jasmine cut her off.

"But James knows all about?" Before Ellie could reply, Jasmine said, "The same James, whom you've known for, what, three days? You could confide in him? But you couldn't confide in me? No offense, James. I'm sure you're a great guy." Jasmine was now standing up from her chair, and so was Ellie. "You know, I've been your best friend, practically your only friend, for how long? No, don't answer that."

Jasmine reached for the takeout she'd brought in, and grabbed her purse she'd left by the door.

Ellie was right beside her, reaching for her shoulder. "Jasmine, wait."

Jasmine dipped down her shoulder, effectively shrugging off Ellie's hand.

"You want me to wait, Ellie? Wait for what? Wait for you to trust me as a friend? I think I've done that and more. I've waited long enough." She looked over her shoulder and called out to me. "Nice meeting you, James." And she walked out the door.

My eyebrows shot up. "What just happened?"

- Ellie

My hands flew to my face and my eyes went wide in shock. "Oh, no. Oh, no. What have I done?" I said to James, then I did what I do. I immediately started pacing.

"Ellie. Tell me what's going on." James said. He stood in the kitchen, looking directly at me.

"Oh, this is bad. This is so bad." I continued to pace. I shook my head, pulled my messy bun down and put it back up. My heart raced and I was breathing hard. This wasn't like what happened yesterday when I freaked out about all the things I needed for EB. This was worse. Much worse.

"I've gathered. Just... just stop for one second and tell me what happened."

I stopped. "I just messed up the one real relationship I have in my life. "

James watched me closely. He was probably trying to figure out if I was going to have another meltdown.

James walked toward me. "Okay, so it sounds like Jasmine is your best friend. Why hadn't you told her about EB?"

"I was going to. I was going to on Monday, probably." I was still walking about the room. "I practically just found out about her myself," I said. "And I didn't tell Jasmine because I didn't have any intention of ever knowing EB, so, what was there to tell? But then I decided to help her, and you know everything from there." I finally stopped walking and looked at James. "I just hadn't gotten to it yet."

He came into the room and sat down on the sofa. "So it sounds like I know more about your life than Jasmine knows, which didn't make her happy, but I'm not sure I know everything. Why did you change your mind about EB? Why did you decide to help her?"

I flopped down onto the sofa, leaned my elbows onto my knees, and put my face in my hands. I stayed like that for a moment, then sat up and turned towards James, angling my leg up on the sofa so I faced him directly. This was the moment. Without Jasmine, I was basically at rock bottom anyway. What did I have to lose?

"By the time I was seven, my dad had disappeared, my mom was a junky, and I was basically raising myself and my sister. I knew at a very young age that we were not important, that we didn't matter to anyone. But that was okay, because I had her, and she had me."

James gave me a small smile. "I'm glad you had—"

"Until foster care." I interrupted. "Within one year of foster care, we were separated. And we were never together again. My parents made it clear my sister and I weren't important, and you don't have to spend much time in the system to find out that all kids are disposable. Just a burden for someone else." I got up and went into the kitchen, and grabbed my glass of wine, the bottle from the fridge, and James's water before I sat back down on the sofa.

James turned toward me and leaned back on the sofa arm. He took a drink of water.

"I decided a long time ago that I would never have kids, and I would never get married. I would never be like my parents. I would never put a family together just to throw it away."

James gave his head a little nod.

"I didn't tell Jasmine about EB, because EB wasn't going to be part of my life. I'm not having kids. I can't be a mother. But then I started thinking. I kept thinking about all of my time in the system, and the very few adults I could count on. And how bad it was. And I thought if I could make it easier on her between now and when she gets placed in a permanent home, I would do that." I took a big gulp of wine. "It's just that all of this has taken place so fast, between finding out about EB, deciding to take her in, meeting you, not being at work, but I really was going to tell her."

"Ah," James replied. "But she doesn't think you were going to tell her?"

I set my glass down on the coffee table. "Right. And for good reason. If you haven't noticed, I'm not one to just gush out all that I'm feeling."

James laughed and reached for my hands. Gosh, I liked it when he did that.

"So she's hurt. You have a lot going on right now, and it seems like you were deliberately keeping her in the dark. And it probably doesn't help that I was here."

I looked him right in the eyes. "No, James, you're wrong. You being here is the only thing that is helping."

Chapter 26

- James

Well, what do you know? I was not expecting that, but I would take it. I liked this girl, and I would take any kind of compliment she'd give. The more I learned about her, the more intriguing I found her. Her life had been hard, but she stood up to it. She fought back. I liked her spark, her backbone. And now I knew why she thought she would never have a family.

I still had her hands in mine. "Then I'm glad I'm here. Not just for the excellent dinner, but for you." I wanted to kiss her. That's what I wanted to do. I could feel myself sway towards her. I could lean in, her lips were right there...

"What am I going to do about Jasmine?" She bit her lip, eyebrows raised, eyes round with concern. Clearly, Jasmine was important to her. Maybe this wasn't the moment for that kiss after all.

I gave her hands a squeeze. "You've been friends for a while. What have you done in the past to get through a rough patch?" Ellie returned the squeeze, stood up from the sofa, and resumed pacing.

"That's the thing. We really haven't had any rough patches. To be honest, sometimes I'm not even sure why Jasmine likes me. Anyone could be her best friend—everyone likes her. People love having her around. She's just so easy. And funny. And fun." Her hands went up to her head, and her hair came down, then went back up.

She stopped pacing and looked at me. "I know I'm difficult. I know I'm hard to get close to. The truth is I'm not interested in sharing my life with just anyone—I barely want to share it with myself."

"You've shared it with me." I held her gaze.

"I have. But you made it easy." She bit her lip. "You make me feel safe."

Dang it. Now I wanted to kiss her again. I needed to focus. This wasn't about me right now.

I stood up. "Okay. Obviously, you'll be seeing each other at work tomorrow. What would normally happen?"

"Normally I'd see her in the break room first thing. I bring in donuts every Monday—and sometimes Wednesdays too. She always joins me there, though we don't always have time to talk."

"You bring in donuts every week?" I asked, my voice filled with surprise.

She burst out laughing. "Well, yeah," she said. "I'm difficult, I'm not stupid. I work with these people. I don't want to share my life story, but I like them. And I want them to like me. It's hard to dislike the girl who brings donuts every week."

Now it was my turn to burst out laughing. "Not for one minute, Dr. Eleanor Dumont, did I think you were stupid. Not one." I grinned.

- Ellie

James and I talked about what I might do to make up with Jasmine, starting with a heartfelt apology. Turns out that James had been *that* kind of big brother—the kind that listened to and helped his little sister with "girl stuff.". She was a lucky girl to have had him for her whole life. I'd just met him and was already thinking I was a lucky girl.

While we talked, all of the items from Target I ordered got delivered, so I washed the sheets and comforter, and James hung up the mirror in EB's bedroom. I'd never thought about how good it might feel to have someone help you. That instead of feeling vulnerable, I would feel safe. I was happy having James help me and I was happy about how the room was coming together. I thought EB was going to like it.

I walked into the room, right as James straightened the mirror above the dresser. I grabbed the lamp off the floor and set it on top, then crouched down to plug it in. I popped back up and looked around. "So what do you think? I think it's really coming together."

James smiled. "I totally agree. I think EB will be happy here."

"Thank you, James. I couldn't have done it without you. I—" but he cut me off before I could continue.

"I don't know about that. You've done a great job of doing things on your own—you would've figured something out. You're good that way." He moved to the door. "It's getting really late, and I have a long drive home, with an early start. I'm going to clean up the kitchen, and then head out." He was gone before I could even reply.

What just happened?

- James

I had to get out of there. I had to get out of there because Ellie was driving me to distraction. The two of us had basically been playing house all weekend, and I couldn't take any more.

Do you know what happens after you've had dinner, set up a bedroom, and cleaned up the kitchen? I know what happens. You watch TV, and then you go to bed. Together. And after the weekend we had shared, going to bed together seemed like exactly the thing to do—and exactly what shouldn't happen.

Ellie came around the corner. "James. Stop. The last thing you have to do is clean up the kitchen. You've done so much for me this weekend already." She put her hand on mine, effectively stopping me where I stood, and moved right next to me. And there we were, side by side, the length of our arms touching when what I wanted was for all of us to be touching. I took a quick step back.

"You know, this time, I'll let you. I really need to go, anyway. I'm just going to grab a water." I moved toward the fridge when Ellie took me completely by surprise.

"James. Don't go." I stopped. I turned around and looked right into her eyes.

She held her hands up. "Just... listen. You've done so much for me this weekend, and I haven't returned the favor in the slightest. And after everything that just went down with Jasmine, the last thing I want to happen is to take you for granted. Maybe you've forgotten, but I haven't. We haven't talked one bit about how I might help you get the bid for the children's wing at the hospital. We could have a drink, a beer, or some wine, and brainstorm some ideas. You could stay the night. In the new bunk beds, or on the sofa if you want." She was quick to point that out. "Then you can get ready here in the morning." She finally paused, after rushing all of that out.

"I don't know." I did want to stay. But did I want to stay with all the temptation that came with it?

"Please. Let me be helpful to you for once. And let me thank you for all that you've done."

Shoot, now my mind was going down the wrong road again. I could think of lots of ways I would like her to thank me.

"Please."

I took a deep breath. I let it out slowly. "Ok. On one condition. You have to have a new toothbrush for me."

She grinned. "On-call doc. I'm always prepared."

And that fast, I was spending the night.

This might be the worst—or the *best*—thing that I ever did.

Chapter 27

- Ellie

I was trying to pull together the things I needed to bring into the office, but I was a little scattered. It seemed like a lifetime had passed since I last went to work, and I was finding it hard to focus.

My apartment looked different.

My apartment felt different.

Heck, *I* felt different.

For how much I'd never wanted a relationship, never wanted anything that would lead to a family, I was definitely acting like it was something I wanted.

James felt worth it. Like maybe I should give this a shot. Maybe? This felt better than how I felt when I thought about my life without him.

The coffee pot was taking forever to finish percolating. Making a whole pot took longer than the single cup serving I usually made. Surely getting some caffeine into me would clear up my head and give me some clarity. I was grateful Mondays were strictly patient appointment days; I wouldn't want to have to perform a procedure right now.

James was in my bathroom taking a shower.

Yes.

That.

Let me restate.

James was in my bathroom taking a shower. That was the true reason for my distraction. I could blame the lack of caffeine all I wanted, but it wouldn't change the truth. I couldn't focus because I could only focus on the fact that he was here, that we had a great weekend together, that he gave me a great hug before we went to bed last night—in separate bedrooms—and now he was taking what I could only imagine was a great shower.

Please, Lord, help me stop imagining.

I finally got everything I needed into my shoulder bag. Today was actually a light day of appointments. I made plans with the Department of Child Services to do their walk-through in the late afternoon. I wanted to have flexibility in my day in case any last-minute things came up, so I rearranged my schedule and appointments to all take place between eleven and two. With all of the work that James and I did this weekend, the walk-through should go smoothly.

Last night I texted Jasmine an apology and asked if we could talk this morning during her break. Mondays tended to be the day she had the most control over her schedule. I also wanted her to know that I would have her very favorite pastry from the Czech Bakery, the bakery I only went to on special occasions. It took her a long time to respond, which was not like her at all, but she finally did. She texted the word 'sigh'. She literally typed the word 'sigh'. And then about 45 minutes later she texted 'fine'.

I was so relieved she was going to meet with me—I needed to apologize to her face to face. I was going to have to grovel. Not because I thought that she would demand that of me, but because I needed her to know I understood how much I'd messed up, and that I wouldn't take her for granted again. I also needed her to know that I trusted her. It was a new feeling for me, but I was willing to try.

Finally. The coffee was ready. I was reaching to pull two cups down from the cabinet when I heard the shower shut off. Just like that, I again lost all focus. Well, rather, I was now focusing on only one thing. After standing there, way too long, doing nothing but thinking all the wrong thoughts, I snapped myself out of it.

I called down the hall. "Hey, James, the coffee is ready. Do you want me to bring you a cup?" That's a thing people do, right? Bring their...friend? Guy friend? Boy who is a friend? Boyfriend? A cup of coffee in the morning after they got out of the shower. Yes. Yes they do, they do exactly that.

I looked down the hall and saw the guest room door was cracked open. Should I just take a little peek in? Bring him coffee and just peek in? That's probably rude, right? Or is it just friendly...

He stuck his head out. Smiled at me. Ah, that smile.

"I would love some coffee. But do you have a to-go mug? 'Cause I really have to get going."

"Yeah, I have a ton of those. Let me get it for you. You want cream or sugar?"

"Nope—just the hard stuff."

"Got it."

I giggled to myself, while I got his coffee ready. *Ah, I loved this!*

Just as I was about to daydream a goodbye kiss with my overnight guest...who was a boy...who was a friend..,, my door buzzer rang and yanked me back to reality. Early morning door buzzes were not typical for me. Stepping over to the intercom, I asked, "Who is it?"

"This is Mrs. Gonzalez with the Department of Child Services. Is this Dr. Dumont?"

"Mrs. Gonzalez? Yes, this is Dr. Dumont. I'm surprised. Our appointment isn't 'til 4:00."

"I"m sorry, and we can keep it at 4:00 if you'd prefer. But I was literally in the neighborhood, and I think our visit will be short. If you could see me now, that would be a huge help to my day."

I knew exactly how overworked caseworkers were, and everything I knew about Mrs. Gonzalez said she was one of the good ones. Which meant she was more than overworked. I'd be happy to be of some help to her day.

"Of course, I'm ready. Fresh pot of coffee, and everything. I'll buzz you right up."

She replied thank you and I pressed the button to open the street side door, then went to my door and opened it. It was funny how excited I suddenly was about this visit. Not much more had to happen in order to get approval to take in EB.

I greeted Mrs. Gonzalez in the hall. "Here. Let me take that for you," I said and reached for one of her oversized bags. I showed her into my apartment.

She stepped into the entryway. "Thank you, Dr. Dumont, this will be a tremendous help to me."

"Please, call me Ellie." I placed her bag on the table by the door and turned to her. "Would you like some coffee?"

"That would be great." She pulled out a clipboard with a pen attached, and a form clipped to the front. "If you don't mind, I'm going to just start checking some things off on my list. It's the same list you were able to retrieve from our website."

"No problem. I'll grab you some coffee." I walked into the kitchen to get her drink when I heard James from the other room.

"Hi. I'm James. I'm sorry, I didn't realize Ellie had company." James.

How had I forgotten about James.?

I rushed around the corner of the kitchen, in time to hear Mrs. Gonzalez. "I'm Mrs. Gonzalez, with the Department of Child Services."

"Oh. That's great. Well, I need to get to work, let me get out of your hair."

Before I could say a word, he grabbed his coffee, leaned down, kissed me on the cheek, and said, "I'll talk to you soon." He moved to the door. "Nice meeting you Mrs. Gonzalez. Good luck, Ellie." And he walked out.

Mrs. Gonzalez looked at me with a big smile on her face. "Well, your boyfriend sure was nice. And handsome."

Wait. What just...what....?

Well, I guess Mrs. Gonzalez called it. I've got a boyfriend.

Chapter 28

- James

I pulled up to the job site. Mario, my foreman, wasn't expecting me today. I could've called him on the drive over and given him a heads-up, but I was busy thinking about Ellie. Thinking about how smart she was. Thinking about how driven she was. Thinking about how strong she was, helping EB. Thinking about her. Period.

"Hey, Boss. Fancy seeing you here." Before I could even slide out of my truck, Mario was at my door. He glanced inside the cab. "No coffee for me this morning?"

"Sorry. Didn't make it by the coffee shop."

"That's okay. I didn't know you were coming, so I stocked up on my own." We walked toward the Walden site. "I take it you're here because of the fireplace issue." We ducked into the back of the home.

The home had a rustic feel to it. Lots of exposed wood and stone throughout the interior. The Waldens wanted a corner freestanding fireplace, but somehow the measurements got turned around and now the fireplace was going to interfere with the accordion glass doors that look out into the backyard. Doors that had already been installed. We were going to have to come up with some solution that made us all happy, or I was going to be eating the cost of those big glass doors.

Mario laid out the blueprint on a makeshift desk of two sawhorses and a piece of plywood so we could discuss the dimensions. It took a bit of time, but we figured out how we could move the fireplace. Not enough to change the feel or layout of the room, but enough to not obstruct the view. I was sure the Waldens would be okay with the change.

"So how did cooking class with the hot doc end up? Any leads for the children's wing?"

I shook my head, rolling up the blueprint. "Hot doc? Is that what we're calling her now?"

"Gotta call her something." Mario was grinning. He was enjoying this a bit too much.

"Ok, then, how about doc. Let's just call her doc."

"Are you saying she's not hot? That's not like you, Boss, every one of your girls has been a looker."

I stopped walking and stared at him. "Every one of my girls? You make it sound like I've got a harem."

"Nah, nothing like that. You're just a serial monogamist."

"Do you even know what that means?"

"I know what it means," Mario fired back. "And when I look it up in the dictionary your picture is next to the definition." We both burst out laughing because it was true. When I dated a girl, I dated her. No wild flings for me.

"So, tell me. Is she hot or not?"

I paused and considered. "She's beautiful."

"Oh man, you like her. I thought you liked her when you mentioned her last week, but now I know you do." Mario was shifting from foot to foot like an overgrown antsy child.

"Why? Why do you think that?" I was curious. What was I doing that made it so obvious that I liked Ellie?

"You just described her as beautiful. You never use that word. You might say it for a new trailer of lumber, or a flat of clay roofing tiles. Heck, I've heard you say it about a piece of meat before you grill it. But otherwise, you use 'pretty.' 'Pretty' is the word you use for girls."

"How long have I known you? 'Cause it's kind of creepy that you know that."

Mario gave me a flat look. "Since we were ten. I have no option but to know that."

I laughed at his comment. "You're right, Mario. I like her." It felt good to say it out loud, and even I could tell this was different. She was different. I wasn't going to follow some rule I put in place for myself about not dating right now just because I put it there. That was the beauty of your own rules—you got to change them. And Ellie was worth the change.

I hit him with the blueprint. "Now get back to work. That thing's not going to build itself."

- Ellie

Mrs. Gonzalez was right—the walkthrough didn't take long at all. I'd gone over the checklist several times, so I knew there wouldn't be any problems—this was practically a formality. Everything on the list was what every home should have. Like a smoke detector and fire extinguisher, as well as a carbon monoxide detector.

She was also checking on general things, like if my home was clean and in good repair. I sure hoped for EB's future home that the standards had gone up since I was in foster care—several of the places I lived would never have been described as 'clean and in good repair.' It made me shudder thinking about it —one of the many reasons I didn't like to think about it.

There were things specific to EB that had to be checked out, as well. She had to have her own bed, with her own bedding and pillow, and it had to be in a room that no adults slept in. Her bed had to be safe—James had made sure the bunk bed with a guard rail for the top bunk wouldn't budge even if there was an earthquake, so that was no problem. And lastly, she made sure that any medications I had would be inaccessible. I didn't have a lot, but I'd purchased a lockable bin for them.

In under thirty minutes, we were back in the kitchen. She even did my formal interview right there on the spot, since we both had the time.

"Thank you so much for accommodating me this morning. Everything is looking good. You know this is an expedited approval process because you're family. So I'll be moving through this as fast as I can." Mrs. Gonzalez was packing up her bag.

"Yes, of course. Let me know what else I can do."

"Let me get back to my office and see what needs to happen next before you can take in your niece. She is very lucky to have you."

"Thank you, Mrs. Gonzalez, you've been such a help to me through this." I picked up her second bag for her. "I'm lucky to have such a caring caseworker."

I opened the door and handed her the bag. She was just about to leave when she turned back to me. "I almost forgot. It was so nice to meet James. Go online to your application and fill out that you have a significant other. It's not necessary that you have one, but a lot of people are still swayed by traditional behavior, and it can only help since you are a single woman making the application. We like to see that people have a support system"

"Oh. Okay." I tried not to let my surprise show. "I'll do that."

With a smile and a wave, Mrs. Gonzalez walked out the door.

It looked like James being my boyfriend was suddenly going to be very official.

And that thought made me feel giddy.

Now how was James going to feel about that?

Chapter 29

- Ellie

I picked up donuts and pastries from the Czech bakery that everyone at the hospital loved—especially Jasmine. She had an affinity for their kolache—a sweet, bread pastry filled with either a meat or a fruit. But she didn't go for the apple or the apricot or some ordinary filling. She went for prune. A prune-filled pastry. Who would've thought?

I was anxious to see Jasmine and get this whole mess I created with her behind us. I dropped the pastries off in the break room, and then brought the small box of kolaches to the nurse's station, searching for Jasmine. She was off to the side, in an animated discussion with Dr. Marks. Great. I didn't want to get in the middle of that, so I caught her eye, lifting the box of kolache up. She nodded her head, which made Marks turn around and give me a look. I walked away before any conversation ensued. He was a reminder of how far behind I was on the Tate project.

My first appointment for the day was with the Woodwards, in about thirty minutes. They had been trying to conceive for over two years, and there was no known reason for why they hadn't. It could be hard on a couple when there was nothing to "fix" in regards to their conception. I'd even seen it tear couples apart, which was the absolute last thing I wanted to be part of. I got into this for people who desperately wanted a family, a family they chose to grow and to grow together.

Luckily the Woodwards were in a very good place. They were even talking about adoption, which I loved. It was often a forgotten option, but one I loved when families did it—such a great way to show a child that they were chosen, that they were wanted—that they were the one. Many children in what was considered a traditional home, didn't even know they were wanted; it was sure made clear to me I wasn't.

Before I went down that road in my mind there was a light tap on the door, and Jasmine walked in. She closed the door behind her and then leaned against it. She let out a big sigh.

"I didn't think Marks was ever going to let me leave. That man can talk." She pushed herself up from the door and headed straight for the bakery box. "These are for me, right?"

"They are. They're all for you." My throat was dry, and I tried to swallow. "Jasmine, I am so sorry about not telling you about my niece. And my sister. And James. And the cooking class." I rushed the apology, wanting to get everything out. Jasmine just stood there, holding her kolache, head tilted to the side.

"Go on," She pulled off a piece of pastry and popped it in her mouth.

"I'm just so sorry. The truth is, I never expected my sister to show up in my life again. When I didn't tell you about her... well, since the falling out we had, I've never told anyone about her."

"But you know I'm not just anyone." Jasmine was firm with her response.

"I do know that."

"I can understand you not telling me about your sister—obviously that's a decision you made a long time ago. But when your niece showed up in your life...?"

"Um, everything was just happening so fast. I had no intention of taking EB in, but once I changed my mind, eight million things happened all at once. I was going to tell you. I was. I just... hadn't."

Jasmine reached for a second kolache. "I know this is a bribe. It's a good one." She pulled off another bite. "So why was it a bad thing, El? Why was I so mad?" She continued to eat, waiting on me. I knew this would be tough, but oh my gosh.

"Because you're my best friend, and I should have told you."

"Why?"

"Because that's what best friends do."

"Why?"

"Because you share things with a best friend."

"Why?"

"Because you...can trust them?"

"Why?"

"Holy cow, Jas, is this an inquisition?"

"No, it's not. I want to make sure you know what you did, and why it's a problem. Why can you trust your best friend? Why can you trust *me*?" Jasmine wasn't eating anymore. She was standing up straight, looking me right in the eye.

I let out an anxious sigh. "Because you look out for me. You always have my back."

"That's true. In all the time I have known you, I have always had your back." Jasmine took a few steps closer to me, wiping her hands on a napkin. "But there are two more things, Ellie, and they might be the most important." Jasmine placed a hand on my arm. "I would never hurt you on purpose. And I'm not going anywhere."

There was a moment of silence, while I stood there. Just stood there, looking at Jasmine, letting that sink in.

"Thank you. I know. I know that about you. And I'm sorry."

"Best friends also forgive each other when one of them sincerely apologizes." She stepped closer and pulled me toward her. "Come here, girl." She gave me a big hug, a hug that I really needed.

She stepped back. "Okay, your apology was good, and so were those kolache. Now, before I go into a sugar coma, tell me. Tell me everything. And start with James."

And so I did.

Where had the day gone? In the end, I was grateful that Mrs. Gonzalez did the walk-through this morning. It allowed me to stay late and catch up on my work after my short week last week. It also made it screamingly obvious how far behind I was on my Tate application. Oddly, I didn't seem to care that much. Today it didn't feel nearly as important as it had a mere seven days ago.

Before heading out, I logged into my application for temporary foster care for EB. I was about to update it with information on James when it occurred to me that maybe I should let him know.

I opened up the messaging app on my phone and dashed him off a text.

Me: Hey, James. As I do - I've got a favor to ask.

Immediately the three moving dots appeared, showing me that he was texting back, and I could feel myself smile.

James: *Hey, back. Anything that you want.*
Me: Mrs. Gonzalez - you met her this morning - suggested you were my boyfriend. And that having a boyfriend would look good on my application. Do you mind if I say you are my boyfriend?

The dots appeared. Stopped. Appeared again. I held my breath. It took a long moment, but then he responded.

James: *I don't mind. But we should make it true. Maybe we should go on a date?*

It was no longer the beginning of a smile on my face—I was grinning from ear to ear.

Me: That would be perfect. I have this weekend off before I'm on-call again.

This time his response was immediate.

James: *I'm not sure I can wait that long.*
Me: What do you have in mind?
James: *I'll come up with something.*
Me: Sounds great. Thanks James
James: *You're welcome. Talk soon.*
Me: :)

And that's how I felt. Like a big ole smiley face emoji.

Chapter 30

- James

Ellie and I were both looking over the menu at Rock Salt Oyster Bar and Grill. Chef Mike suggested it to me, and I knew Ellie liked seafood, so I thought it would be a hit. It had only been open for about six months, and it was getting a lot of buzz. When I told Ellie they had a 'raw oyster happy hour' before seven pm, she scrambled to wrap up her day so we could make it in time. Our waitress had just delivered our first dozen oysters.

Ellie loaded up her oyster with hot sauce. I opted for straight lemon juice. I held up my first oyster in its shell like it was a drink. "To cooking classes that lead to...well, that lead to more." Suddenly I was self-conscious, not sure how what I'd said might be received.

Ellie held up her oyster and grinned. "To more." She was emphatic in her statement; she liked my toast. We both slurped down our oysters and reached for seconds.

"So how did your talk with Jasmine go?" I asked.

"Good, it was good. Thank goodness she's so good at friendships. She did hold my feet to the fire a bit. She made sure I really understood what I did."

"And did you? Understand what you did?" I reached for more lemon.

"It took a minute, but yeah. Just like we talked about last night, she felt like I didn't trust her. And if I don't trust her, there's really not a foundation for our relationship. For any relationship, for that matter. And I know better about Jasmine. I can definitely trust her. Thanks for talking through it with me last night."

"Of course. It sounds like your apology worked. What about the walk-through with Mrs. Gonzalez? How did that end up?"

"Great. We did the interview, too. I'd gone over the checklist ahead of time, so she just had to verify that everything met the standards. There weren't any surprises."

"Other than me being your boyfriend."

"Right. That. Thanks again for agreeing to that. Right before Mrs. Gonzalez left she said my application might come across stronger if I could show a support system. And since she already thought you were my boyfriend, it seemed like the natural thing to do." Ellie blushed a bit at that statement, so I quickly reassured her.

"I can think of a lot of things worse than being your boyfriend, Ellie."

Ellie burst out laughing, and I joined her when I realized how that sounded.

"Let me try again. I'm happy to be your boyfriend. And besides, look at us. Here we are taking the first steps in that direction."

Ellie raised an eyebrow and gave me a little grin. "That, we are."

Just that little grin and adrenaline shot through me.

I felt like I was falling.

This girl.

Suddenly, all I wanted was for dinner to be over, so I could get to the good night kiss. Because there was going to be a good night kiss. There had to be.

We were wrapping up our meal, and then Ellie ordered dessert. Dang it. Doesn't she know I am trying to get out of here? I was mostly a patient man, but this evening was testing me. I reached for my beer, knowing we were going to be a little bit longer.

"I had to try their triple chocolate cake. I'm pretty sure it won't compare to our chocolate lava cake, but I had to know. I want to bask in the glory of mastering that recipe. I'm feeling like if I can do that, I can do anything."

I laughed out loud at her comment and put down my beer. "You deliver babies for a living. You solve complex fertility issues. You perform surgery. But it's mastering chocolate lava cake that proves you can do anything?" I shook my head back and forth and grinned at her. The girl did make me smile.

"Well, yeah. I can already do those things." She gave me a smirk and handed me the extra fork the waitress had brought with the cake. "Let's see if we have any competition." She took a big bite.

I quickly followed, raising my eyebrows as I swallowed. "What do you think?"

"Let me try again." She took a second bite. "It's good. But it's no lava cake."

"I think you mean it's no 'Ellie's super-spectacular-hand-crafted-chocolate-lava-cake.' 'Cause you're right. It's good—but it's not as good as yours."

She clapped her hands in delight. "I win, I win."

I laughed out loud. "And to think, they didn't even know they were competing."

Ellie laughed and then took a few more bites of the cake. She pushed it towards me. "Oh, they knew. Everything is a competition."

I wasn't sure I agreed, but I could go with it.

Finally, dinner was over, and I closed out the tab. As we walked towards my truck, I took Ellie's hand in mine. For the many times I'd wanted to reach for her and hadn't, especially for fear of moving too fast, this felt natural. This felt right. Like we were supposed to be the happy-couple-walking-down-the-sidewalk together, hand in hand.

Ellie gave my hand a little tug. "Oh, I meant to tell you. Since you are my boyfriend on my foster application," she gave me a quick look, "someone will probably contact you for an interview. I don't think it's anything in-depth, since listing people isn't even a requirement. But they'll want to do a background check, make sure you're not a criminal."

We had just reached my truck, and I opened the passenger door for her, continuing to stand in the doorway as she sat down, legs still a bit out of the car, not having turned completely into the seat "It's taking everything in me right now not to joke that I am a criminal. But the timing isn't right. I'm pretty sure you wouldn't appreciate it."

Ellie's eyes narrowed for a brief moment. "You're right. I wouldn't appreciate that."

I stepped a bit closer to where she was seated. I'd been waiting for this moment all night. Or for many days, depending on how you count. "You know what else is taking everything in me not to joke about right now?"

Ellie's eyes flared wide. "What?" Her voice was quiet when she asked.

"Kissing you. I'm definitely not joking about that. Can I kiss you, Ellie?" I realized I was holding my breath. This was hard to do since my heart was pounding so hard it was crowding into my lung space.

"Yes. Yes, you can. That is something I would appreciate."

I slowly let out my breath, which didn't slow down my racing heart. I reached for her, sliding one palm along her cheek, and then... I leaned in.

And I kissed Dr. Eleanor Dumont.

- *Ellie*

James was kissing me. And oh, what a kiss. My eyes closed of their own accord as his lips landed on mine, soft yet firm. He kissed like the James I'd come to know—with patience, and with kindness. I could tell he wanted to deepen the kiss, but he waited, waiting for me.

The palm of his right hand was resting on my cheek, with his fingertips pushed into my hair. With the tip of my tongue, I touched his lower lip. His thumb moved slowly across the crest of my cheek, and his left hand moved from the truck frame that he had been leaning on to my other cheek. Chills raced up my spine, and goosebumps rushed down my arms.

James moved in closer and stepped between my knees. I could feel his thighs brush against mine. All I wanted was to get closer. How could I get closer?

My heart was pounding, and the world narrowed to just the two of us.

He angled my head to the side while framing my face with his hands, and his tongue moved between my lips. He was definitely in control of this kiss, yet he was making it clear that the control could be mine if I wanted it.

I moved my arms to circle his neck and pulled him towards me when someone called out, "Get a room." Some low laughter followed the comment.

James gently bit my lower lip and pulled, scraping his teeth lightly as he moved back and away. Our kiss ended, lips falling apart. James rested his forehead against mine and kept his right hand on my cheek. That thumb continued to slowly stroke, and I could feel the slight callus there. Gosh, how I loved his hands.

He gave me a soft smile.

"Too much?" he asked.

"Too perfect."

"That sounds about right." He pressed one more kiss to my lips and reached for the door. "Let's get you home." He waited for me to get situated, then walked around the front of the truck.

No matter how much I hated to admit it, he was right. It was time to go home.

But it didn't have to be all bad. Because maybe, if I was lucky, I'd get a goodnight kiss at the door.

A girl could hope.

Chapter 31

- Ellie

James: *Do you have a couple of minutes this morning to talk?*

It was a simple text from James at the start of my morning, but oh, what a start.

Me: I have thirty minutes between 9:30 and 10
James: *Great. I'd like to come to your office and talk to you.*

I was surprised. So happily surprised.

Me: Ok! Sounds good! See you soon.
James: *See you.*

James was at my office right on time. I'd left the door open because frankly, I didn't want to miss one second with him. He leaned in, knocking on the door frame.

I stood up from my desk and wiped my hands down the front of my skirt. Was I nervous to see James? I think I was nervous! That good, giddy kind of nervous.

"James. Hi. How nice to see you in the middle of my morning. I could get used to this," I said.

Because I could, I realized.

I pulled up a chair. "Here, have a seat."

"Hi." He walked into the room but didn't sit down. "I'll make this quick. I know how hard you've been working for EB, and I didn't want to have this conversation over the phone."

Wait. That didn't sound good.

James inhaled deeply, then said, "Mrs. Gonzalez called me today."

"And?" I tilted my head to the side and waited to see what was so concerning.

"She called to set up an appointment to interview me for your application."

"Right. I mentioned that to you last night."

"But you didn't mention last night that you said we lived together."

I straightened my spine. "What? I never said we lived to-gether. I..."

Oh my gosh, I *did* say we lived together. When I filled out the guardian form, it asked for James's address. There was a "click this box" if the address is the same as yours, so I clicked it thinking I would just fill it in later. I completely forgot to come back to it.

Cautiously I asked, "What happened then?"

"She wanted to meet at your"— he waved between us— "which you said was *our* apartment. I told her I wanted you to be there, too, so I needed to check with your schedule and get back to her. I'm not sure what to do now."

"Oh." I shook my head, clearing my thoughts. "You scared me for a minute there." I could fix this. This was easy. "I know exactly what to do. We make it look like you live with me, and we have the interview. Problem solved."

We could do this. I leaned back against my desk.

James hesitated, and he was *not* smiling. "I'm not sure that solves the problem. In fact, I think that makes the problem worse."

"Why?" I was confused. "She thinks you live with me. It's super easy to make it look like we live together, right? We can just throw some of your clothes in a closet and a drawer or whatever, right?" I could feel my stomach knotting up. Why didn't he want to do this for me?

James blew out a big breath of air and stuffed both of his hands in his front pockets.

"Ellie, I don't think you are thinking this through."

"Not thinking? All I've been doing is thinking about this. *Non-stop*. Since I found out about EB." The knot was turning to panic. Didn't he know how badly I wanted this now? "I don't understand why this is a big deal. I'm not actually asking you to move in with me. I just think it will make this a lot easier if we make it look like that. I just want to get this process over with. What is so complicated about that?"

I walked back around my desk and sat down. This conversation was getting really frustrating and I needed to get control.

"Aside from the fact that it's not true. I don't think you're thinking about the long-term effect," he said. "What about when your application is approved and she brings EB to your home, and I don't live there?"

I threw my hands up. "I don't know! I'll tell her we broke up." What wasn't he getting about this? I needed this to work with EB. It had to.

"Ellie. Listen to what you're saying. Listen to yourself."

"I *am* listening to myself!" I felt my voice start to rise. Now I wasn't just frustrated by this conversation, I was also frustrated with James. Didn't he know how hard this was? Didn't he know what a huge leap I was taking? I'd never planned on taking in EB. But now I wanted her more than anything. If I was being honest with myself, he was part of the reason I wanted this. He had been so helpful up to this point. Oh my gosh, that was it. As soon as I relied on someone for help, this is what I got. All this pushback and conflict—I didn't need this. I should never have done this.

"You're right," I said. "I need to listen to myself. And listen to what I have always known to be true. I should have just done this by myself like I've done everything in my life."

James gave his head a little shake.

"Now *I* don't know what *you're* saying," he said.

I stood up from my chair and put my fingertips on the top of my desk.

"I'm saying thanks for trying to help me. But I'll take it from here."

James took a step closer to my desk. His eyebrows were pulled down and in, and he was frowning. Hard.

"You'll take *what* from here?"

"Don't worry about it, James." I waved my hand. "You're totally right. We don't live together. I'll call Mrs. Gonzalez, I'll clear everything up. You're off the hook."

James took another step closer and held up both his hands.

"Wait. I was never on the hook. I wanted to help. I wanted—"

I cut him off. I didn't need explanations.

"I know, James. You wanted to help. I got it. Like I said, I've got an appointment at ten I need to get ready for. It's a wonder you caught me when you did. You can see yourself out."

He just stood there. Waiting.

"Ellie," he finally said. "This isn't over."

I stood firm.

"It is. Goodbye James."

He gave it another beat, and then he turned and walked out.

I fell back in my chair and threw my hands over my face.

It *felt* like it was over.

It really felt like it was over.

I called Mrs. Gonzalez and asked her to meet James and me at my apartment tomorrow night for his interview. Of course, he wouldn't be there, but I would clear everything up with her then. I needed to get things back on track, especially now that I was doing this without James.

I was doing this without James.

My stomach did a slow churning flip-flop.

I had a full schedule of appointments ahead, but first I had to talk to Jasmine. I needed to let her know what was going on so that I didn't blindside her again. More than anything, I needed her to be on my side.

I went down to the nurse's station to check her schedule and found her and Dr. Marks, off to the side, once again in a heated discussion.

"Jasmine. Marks. Can I talk to Jasmine for a minute?" I rudely interrupted, but I was guessing Jasmine would want that. I wanted that.

"Ellie! Of course. What do you need?" Jasmine turned her back on Dr. Marks, and he shook his head, then walked away without a word.

"What was that all about?" I was suddenly curious about what would have the two of them in such a heated conversation. Plus, thinking about them meant I wasn't thinking about James.

"You know that man. It's always something with him. What's going on with you? How was the date?" Jasmine's eyes were wide, and she seemed distracted. Marks must really be bugging her these days.

"Shoot. The date." I rubbed my temples. How did it feel like an eternity ago? "So much has happened since the date."

"What? Wasn't the date last night?"

"Yeah, it was," I said. "But I think we just broke up. We really just broke up."

"Hold. The phone. What's going on?" Jasmine looked confused. I didn't blame her.

"The date was great. It really was. But you know how I told you I put James on EB's foster application?"

"Yesss..."

"I accidentally said he lived with me, too. I mean, I checked the box that said we lived at the same address. I didn't have his address, and I just wanted to get the application finished. I planned on going back and fixing it, but everything is just happening so fast. And then he was all weird about it, so I told him I didn't want his help. And I think we broke up."

Jasmine stared at me. For one long moment. Then she said, "James, the great guy, who after knowing you for a minute was helping you build bunk beds."

"Oh yeah, he loves to help," I said while rolling my eyes.

Jasmine put her hands on her hips. "The same James who then said it was okay to say he was your boyfriend, and then made it true by taking you on a date."

"Yes." She didn't seem to be getting this either.

"The same James who took you on that date—that you just said was great—that same James—is now being weird and broke up with you?"

I suddenly felt a lot less sure of myself. I didn't love where she was going with this. I reached for the messy bun on top of my head. Shoot. I wore my hair down today. "Well..."

"Ohhh, no." Jasmine shook her head slowly back and forth. "*You* were being weird and broke up with *him*."

Yep. Definitely didn't love where she went.

"Well, only kind of. I mean, he wouldn't tell Mrs. Gonzalez he was living with me." Now I sounded like I was pouting.

"Of course, he wouldn't say that." Jasmine threw her hands up and dropped them down by her side. "He isn't living with you."

"But he should say... that..." I trailed off and peered down the hall. Anything to not be looking at Jasmine.

"Should he really?"

I turned back to her.

"Suddenly that seems like a rhetorical question," I said.

Jasmine raised her eyebrows. "It is."

I started pacing. And pacing. I walked past Jasmine once, twice, and the third time, I stopped. She was right. He was right. They were both right. My "solution" was ridiculous. "I'm an idiot," I said.

"I'm not arguing."

"I know how good James is. I know it. We've already established that. He has already established that. Why am I such an idiot?"

"I can't answer that."

"What should I do? Oh my gosh, what should I do?"

"This doesn't have to be all convoluted and filled with drama." Jasmine stood in front of me and took both my shoulders in her hands. "This is just your first fight. Your first argument. Couples do that. Just call him. Tell him you're not used to this whole trustworthy relationship thing and apologize. Tell him you're wrong and you see the error of your ways." She paused. "Tell him you want his help."

I bit my lip. "Of course, I want his help. I think it's clear I want more from him than just help. But how do I tell him, especially after what just happened?" My stomach was swooping all over the place. Not with the feeling of butterflies, but more like the feeling of a tsunami.

"You just do. You suck it up, and you tell him you made a mistake. 'Cause that's what people in a relationship do."

I stood still and took a deep breath. I was feeling better already.

"Okay. I'll do it. I'll do it. Thanks. I'll talk to you later."

I spun to walk away—I had that ten o'clock—then turned back. "Hey. You still need to tell me what's going on with Marks, too."

But she was already down the hall, onto something else.

Chapter 32

- Ellie

James was sitting at my kitchen table, watching me. I'd taken Jasmine's advice and called him. After thoroughly apologizing—I was getting pretty good at it—he had agreed to be with me when I met with Mrs. Gonzalez tonight. I was sure I could clear up everything, but I was anxious to get it over with, so I could move on with the next steps. Therefore, I was pacing.

I buzzed up Mrs. Gonzalez when she got to my apartment, thankful I didn't have to wait long.

"Hi. Thanks so much for meeting with us so quickly." I ushered her into my home.

"You're welcome. I wanted to speak with you, as well."

"Okay, good." I dove right in. "There's something I need to clear up."

"What is that?" Mrs. Gonzalez asked.

"James doesn't live with me. He has his own place."

"I see."

"When I updated the online application to include James, I checked the box that said we lived at the same address. I didn't have his address, and I just wanted to get the application updated. I planned on going back and fixing it, but everything is just happening so fast. I honestly never thought about it again until James told me his interview was going to be held here."

Mrs. Gonzalez raised her eyebrows. "So you don't know your boyfriend's address?"

"Well, no. We're kind of new." I looked at James. He was sitting there, giving me all the silent support I needed to keep going. "But as you can see...he's here. We're together. It's important enough that we both thought he should be on the application. I was so focused on getting things done so EB could be placed with me as quickly as possible, that I forgot about fixing his address."

Finally. This felt good. It felt right. No lying, no twisting the truth. I wanted to keep this process moving. I knew that James's interview would go well, and we would wrap things up quickly. I was so excited to finally get to meet EB.

"Ah. I see. That explains a lot."

Wait. That didn't sound good. It had the same feeling to it that my conversation with James had yesterday. And that conversation did not go well.

"What do you mean that explains a lot?"

"I mean that will go a long way when we resubmit your application in six weeks," she said.

My stomach dropped straight to the floor.

"Six weeks? I thought we were almost finished with this. I thought interviewing James would be the last step. I thought maybe I would get EB like...soon. Like, this weekend soon."

My world was screeching to a halt.

"Ellie, I'm sorry. I wanted to see you because there was a problem with your application. James's address was the problem."

"But what do you mean? I just explained that to you. It was a mistake. We just told you."

"You know this was a fast track application because you're a relation. We already did James's background check. Everything was checking out, except his address. There was no proof that he lived at this address. In fact, there was a lot of proof that he lives at a different address. And because I'd already done the walk-through, I already saw that he didn't live here. It raised a red flag"

I felt like stone, a statue, like I wouldn't be able to move from this spot.

"But...I don't know, couldn't we have broken up? People break up, don't they? Can't we say we broke up and he moved out and he's not even my boyfriend anymore?" I took in a big gulp of air, trying to breathe. "Or something?" I knew I sounded absurd, but I felt desperate. Desperate to make this happen.

"Surely you can see why that wouldn't work."

"Surely you can see why me quickly clicking on a button shouldn't prevent me from caring for my niece." I knew I sounded snippy, but I couldn't believe this was happening. This couldn't be happening.

"It's not. It's just delaying it. That kind of conflicting in-formation freezes an application. I understand that it was a mistake, but it was a mistake that has already generated the next step. It could be considered falsifying government documents. That's why we have to be so careful. But don't worry, I can still interview James and have everything ready. We'll be right at this point, and we should be able to move EB in quickly."

My voice was flat when I spoke. It held no emotion. Just like I felt. Numb. "Except for the part where six weeks has gone by."

"Well, yes," Mrs. Gonzalez replied. "But we'll find a good home for her in the meantime."

My head was spinning, while the rest of me remained numb. "What's next?" I wasn't sure why I was even asking. It was clear this was over.

"I'll interview James, at his home, and we'll just need to resubmit your application in six weeks."

"Okay." This wasn't okay. It wasn't going to ever be okay.

I moved to hold the door for Mrs. Gonzalez, and she walked out, patting my arm. "It'll work out, Ellie. Don't worry."

I nodded my head and closed the door behind her.

Then I walked to the sofa, sat down, and burst into tears.

- James

I rushed to Ellie and joined her on the sofa. She was crying. Silently crying. Not a sound was made as big tears fell from her eyes. And it was killing me.

"Ellie. What can I do? What can I do to help?"

She leaned over, her face in her hands, and rocked. I slowly rubbed my hand up and down her back, at a loss for anything else to do.

She didn't answer for some time. And then, I got exactly what I was beginning to expect from Ellie. Face still buried in her hands, she said, "Nothing. There's nothing you can do."

"I know you're upset. But six more weeks isn't that long. And we can—"

She shot off of the sofa, and her eyes flashed.

"I know you're trying to help, but this isn't about *we*, James. This is about me. Six weeks is an eternity in foster care. Anything can happen in six weeks. Six days, even. Heck, it only takes six minutes for something awful to happen.."

I waited. Sitting silently on the sofa.

"I'm doing this to EB. I'm the reason she's going to be in that position. Because I couldn't do it right. I couldn't get her out." She let out a little sob. "It's happening again. Just like with my sister."

I approached this cautiously. "Just like what with your sister?"

She froze. Stock still.

"Nothing. It's nothing. You should go. This was a stupid idea, it was all a stupid idea. I've been so stupid. I told you I could never be a mother. I told you. I don't know how I talked myself into this."

Ellie stopped crying and stood up from the couch. She walked to the door and pulled it open. I stayed right where I was. It was going to take a lot more than an open door to get me to leave.

"Tell me what happened with your sister."

"No."

"I don't get it. What happened with your sister that feels like what's happening with EB? You impulsively checked off a box on a form. You had no idea it would delay your application. People do much more impulsive things than that all the time. Heck, I just did something the other day, on an impulse. It's just a moment. It'll be okay."

"It's not just a moment. It's so many moments. And it didn't turn out okay. I tried and tried and tried to get my sister and me into the same home. So I could take care of her. So I could look out for her. And I couldn't do it. It didn't matter who I talked to. Over and over again I was told maybe next month. Just try again next month. Or maybe the month after that. But it never happened. I could never do it. Just like I can't do this."

I stood up. "Oh, Ellie." She looked so fragile. "I'm not sure that was you 'not doing it.' You were a kid. There were rules in place. Kids aren't supposed to be taking care of other kids. That's not how it works. It's not the same thing."

"It's exactly the same thing. I threw away my sister. And now I just threw away EB. Just like my mother. I'm just like my mother."

"You didn't. You didn't th—" I reached out to her but she held her hands up.

"I need you to leave James. Thanks for your help, but I need you to go. I need some time. I need some space. I don't need..." She waved her arms around. "This. I don't need this."

"Ellie, I know you don't mean that. Just like you didn't mean it yesterday morning."

She didn't even blink.

"I do. You should go."

I wanted to fight. I wanted to fight everything she was saying. More than that, I wanted to hold her. I wanted to hold her and do whatever I could to help her feel better, so she would look at this differently. But there was no fighting her on this. She was done. It was clear in her eyes, and by the set of her face. I needed to walk away.

This time, when she waved her hand through the doorway, I followed.

"I'll call you," I said, but she just stood there. Not even a nod. "We'll figure something out."

I kissed her on the cheek, then turned and walked out. She was upset, and I didn't know how all of this would work, but I knew one thing for sure.

I wasn't throwing out Ellie.

Chapter 33

- James

It had been two full days since I'd left Ellie's, and she was not answering my calls or returning my texts.

I was desperate to know what was going on with her, so I hunted down Jasmine at the hospital, to make sure she was okay. I'd never gone to such extremes over a girl before. I'd never been so twisted up over a girl before. It didn't surprise me when Jasmine didn't share anything specific. All she would say was that she was worried about Ellie, too, and that she didn't seem to be acting like herself.

Mrs. Gonzalez had reached out to interview me like she said she would. She wanted to keep Ellie's application updated, so it would be ready to go when the six week hold was over. I went ahead with the interview, though I wasn't certain that Ellie would even go through with fostering EB.

She was so convinced that she could never be a mother. That she could only be like her own mother. She couldn't see how wrong she was.

I stopped by my family's home, hoping to catch a moment with my sister.

I quietly entered the house and found Lizzy on the sofa, feet up on the coffee table, head leaned back with her eyes closed. There was a bag of diapers spilled over on the floor, and a couple of baby blankets heaped in a pile next to her.

"What?" She didn't open her eyes. "Can't you see I'm trying to sleep here?"

"I didn't even say anything."

"You didn't have to. Mothers hear everything. I can hear you breathing."

"You're not my mother."

She opened one eye. "Not *your* mother, dummy. *A* mother. James's mother. Not *you*, James, but ... oh for goodness sake, I'm so tired I'm not even making sense."

She sat up, rubbed her hands over her face, and looked around the room.

"Are you looking for something?" I asked.

"I was hoping a cup of coffee would magically appear."

"Right after you called me dummy?"

"I've called you worse."

"That, you have. Stay there. I'll get it for you. Cream and sugar?" I moved towards the kitchen.

"Yes, please. Thank you, James. You're one of the good ones."

I got my sister her coffee and came back to the room.

"So what are you doing here on a random weekday? It is a weekday, right?" she asked as she searched for her phone. "This is unusual."

I handed my sister her coffee, and she wrapped her hands around the mug. She took a big swallow and sighed with contentment.

"It's been an unusual kind of week," I said.

"Do tell."

"It's about Ellie."

"Of course it is."

"What do you mean by that?"

"She's an unusual girl. Remember? Different. You've been different about her. So what's going on?" She took another drink.

I brought Lizzy up to speed with everything that had happened since we last spoke. Except for the part about that kiss. That incredible kiss.

"I've got mere minutes before that nephew of yours is demanding all of my attention. So what are you gonna do?"

"That's the thing. I'm not sure what to do."

"I bet you have some ideas. But try this. How about you do the opposite of what you would have done with any of your past girlfriends."

Why was she bringing up old girlfriends? "What do you mean?"

"How did all of those other relationships start and end? With all those girls who could have been 'the one.' And definitely weren't?"

"I haven't thought about it," I said. "Most of them started because they approached me, I guess. I didn't have to do anything. We just became a couple.."

She raised an eyebrow. "And why did they end?"

"I guess because...we...I don't know. They just ended." I shrugged.

Lizzy put her coffee cup down. "Let me give it a shot. They approached you. You didn't have to do anything. It was easy." She paused, still looking at me with exasperation. "Easy come, easy go."

"Yeah," I said. "But you make it sound bad. I did actually like those women."

"Did you really? Or did you like having a relationship?"

I grabbed the napkin I brought in with Lizzy's coffee and tore it in frustration. I'd never thought of it that way. "I don't know."

"So what are you going to do differently? Your other girlfriends coasted right into your life and then coasted on out, even after they hung around for quite a while. Nothing about Ellie has sounded like that. She sounds like she challenges you. She sounds like she makes you think. Actually, James, it sounds like she's knocked you off your game. And I mean that in a good way."

I chuckled. "That's pretty accurate." I slowly shredded the napkin. "I don't know what I'm going to do. And I'm going out of my mind trying to figure it out. At least I know what she's upset about. It's not even me she's mad at. Though I'm not sure she knows that."

"James, you're a good guy. I mean that. You care about—and *for*—everyone. Everyone who knows you can't believe that you are 35 and not married. So why is that?"

I threw the napkin down on the coffee table and ran both my hands through my hair. "I don't know," I stated with emphasis.

"You have the biggest heart of anyone I know. But did you ever give even a piece of it to any of those women? Did you ever go out on a limb and take a real risk? Something beyond what you would do for just anyone?" She softened her voice. " Maybe you should think about that."

"Why did Mom and Dad have to make this look so easy? You find the one and boom. Everything just happens. That's what I've been looking for."

Lizzy laughed, and it wasn't long until tears were running down her face. "Oh, James. If you've been looking for 'boom—and everything just happens,' you're going to be looking for a lot longer."

She grabbed the last of the napkin from the table and wiped her cheek. "Real relationships take effort . They don't just magically work. But when it's the right person, the work is worth it."

I sat there and took that in. From the other room, baby James cried out. Lizzy stood up from the sofa.

"So is she worth it? That's the question."

Was she? Maybe if I gave her more than I gave anyone else, took a risk, like Lizzy said, she'd be able to let down some of her walls. Heck, I built walls for a living, but often you had to tear some stuff down before you started. I could do this work. Together, we could demolish her walls, and whatever I'd been using for protection, too.

"I think she is," I said.

"Then I think you'll know what to do." Lizzy leaned down and gave me a quick hug, and then she was gone.

I stood up and headed for the door. "I think I do," I said to no one, and walked out, putting together my plan.

- Ellie

I'd been doing what I always did when faced with something I didn't want to face. I'd been working. A lot. And doing research for the Tate. A lot. But I was just going through the motions. All I could think about was how I'd failed EB. Just like I'd failed my sister.

Jasmine found me in my office, leaned back in my chair, staring out the window. She walked in on tiptoes, careful to not make any sudden movements like I was her most fragile patient. Maybe I was.

"Hey." She whispered as she closed the door softly behind her.

"Hey," I replied, flatly.

"Soo, watcha doin'?" Jasmine used a sing-song voice, like the lightness in her tone would transfer to me. It didn't.

She grabbed a chair and pulled it over in front of my desk. I didn't bother to move. I couldn't bother. Nothing mattered.

"I know you're upset, Ellie, but you've got to snap out of this."

"I don't, actually. I've got my work. I've got the Tate Award research due at the end of next week. I'll be fine."

I'd told Jasmine everything that happened with me and my sister, and with Mrs. Gonzalez and my messed up application. It was incredibly humiliating to admit how badly I'd failed. Again.

"It's been days, and even though I know you love your work, you have barely left the hospital. Did you even go home last night?"

"I don't need to go home. I've got things here. I can get ready in the locker room."

"Ellie, drowning yourself in work isn't going t—"

"It's all I've got. It's all I've had. It's got to be enough. I've got to make it enough."

Jasmine got out of her chair, walked around the front of my desk, and leaned on the corner, encroaching in my space. I didn't like it.

"Work is not enough. And it's not all you have. You have me. If you would try, I bet you could still have James. You'll have EB soon. You need to go home tonight and—"

"I only have you. And work. I don't have anything else. And I can't go home. I can't go there."

"Why? Why can't you go there?"

"Because nothing is there. It's just empty, except for one room, filled with everything a little girl might need. A little girl that will never be there."

"But that doesn't have to be true. You can still get EB. Even Mrs. Gonzalez said—"

"I can't. I can't get her. I tried and I failed. Again. I'm so tired of trying and failing." I was tired of the constant churning in my gut, too.

"You can get her. In six weeks—"

"In six weeks, nothing. I've been turned down. It's over. I'm done. It was all going to be temporary anyway. I never should have gotten involved."

Jasmine stood straight up, grabbed my hands, and pulled me to my feet.

"There's a time to wallow, and there's a time for action. You've felt sorry for yourself long enough. There's a little girl out there that needs you. Not just someone. She. Needs. You." Jasmine's lips were pulled tight into a thin line, her brows furrowed. I'd seen that look before. She used it when she was working with a particularly stubborn patient. But I wasn't being stubborn, I was being realistic.

"Not true," I said. "I just proved it. I couldn't even get through the application process." I could feel exhaustion creeping over me just thinking about it.

"Ohh, I want to shake you," Jasmine said. "You're a renowned fertility doctor, for goodness sake. You are so far from being a failure it is not even funny. Every day you help people make a family. You have an opportunity to make one right now, and you're not going to?"

"Exactly. I am great at helping other people make a family. As long as it's not mine. Just look what I did to my sister. Look what I did to EB."

"You didn't—" Jasmine cut herself off. Shook her head. "You're just going to walk away?"

I stood there, not answering. She knew my answer.

Jasmine took a deep breath and walked to the door. She reached for the handle and turned back to me.

"Go home. Think about what you are doing. Think about what it means if you walk away from EB right now. There are people in your corner, Ellie, even if you don't think so."

Jasmine left me in my office. Alone. Like I'd always liked it.

Though, I wasn't so sure anymore.

Because I didn't like this at all.

Chapter 34

- Ellie

I went home. I picked up some dinner on the way —it seemed like years since the cooking class—and I walked straight into EB's room. I sat on the floor, pulled out my chopsticks and Chinese food, and leaned back against the wall. And then I took it all in.

I thought about the phone call when I found out about my sister and my niece. About how I had no intention of taking EB in. How I'd changed my mind and decided to temporarily care for her, and tried to build the bunk beds by myself.

My stomach twisted in knots.

I thought of how James had jumped in to help and then watched my meltdown when I realized I didn't have everything EB was going to need.

How he stuck around, helping me out with the rest of the furniture, even after I'd been hot and cold in cooking class. How he had taken me out on a date—*that date*—and how he had kissed me like he meant it.

And then how I'd just... I'd just...thrown it all away.

Just. Like...

I jumped to my feet. My gosh, I really was an idiot. What was it that Jasmine had said? "There were people in my corner, even if I didn't think so." It was being proven to me over and over again—it was time to believe it. Right now.

I called Mrs. Gonzalez and left her a message. And then I called both Jasmine and James. I had some explaining to do.

James was meeting me at the bar at SoBo. When I walked in, I was immediately transported back to our cooking classes, and how much fun we had. I was hoping that meeting in the place where we got to know each other would do the same for him. I needed all the help I could get when I tried to convince him not to give up on me.

When I saw him walk into the bar, my stomach flipped over, and my hands began to sweat. I couldn't remember the last time I'd been so nervous. And I'd been nervous a lot, lately. I felt like it was the first time I was performing surgery, life or death, with the outcome still to be determined, not to be revealed until the very end.

Only this time, I was not nearly as prepared. Fighting for a relationship was still new to me, even considering the talk I'd just had with Jasmine. I hadn't done it since I fought for my sister so many years ago. But I was doing it now. For James. And ultimately EB.

I stood up when James approached the table and I motioned to his chair. I wanted to hug him, but I didn't think I could start there. I'd ordered water and drinks for us and had asked the waiter not to stop back by until we called for him. I didn't want to be interrupted in the middle of our talk. James slipped into his seat and gave me a small smile. And before I could speak, he jumped right in.

"So what's going on, Ellie?" He reached for his napkin and pulled it into his lap. "I told you on the phone I was surprised to hear from you after you had been dodging my calls and texts."

"You are so right. I was dodging you. I was wrong. And I'm sorry."

"Yeah?" James took a drink of his water and barely looked at me.

I knew this was going to be hard. Maybe harder than when I'd apologized to Jasmine. Definitely harder than when I'd apologized to Jasmine.

"I messed up. I messed up everything. I freaked out about losing EB, and—"

James cut me off and sat straight up in his chair. "You're still saying you lost EB. When are you going to see—"

This time I cut him off.

"No. No, you're right. You and Jasmine were both right. I made a mistake. I hate it, and I hate that it puts EB into an unknown situation, but throwing her into an unknown situation because of a mistake is not the same as throwing her away by choice. Which I was so close to doing. And I couldn't even see it."

He leaned back in his chair.

"I was this close to walking away from her." I scoffed. "I was done, and I was never going to reapply to foster her. I don't know how I could have been so stupid. And selfish. I should know better than anyone how much that child needs me. And I don't know if I would've seen it without you and Jasmine."

I took a deep breath.

"Have I ever told you why I became a doctor?"

He shook his head. "You haven't."

"Because I wanted to help. I couldn't help my sister, so I thought I could help other kids. And then I got into obstetrics." I reached for my water glass and pulled it close to me.

I looked up at James. "I love kids. I love families. All I ever wanted was a big, happy family. And I figured since I would never have one of my own, at least I could help people who wanted one as much as I did."

James had a small smile on his face, but he remained quiet.

"You may have noticed," I said, and slowly spun my water glass. My nerves were still with me. "I'm a bit quick on the draw to respond to personal things, and not always in the best way."

James chuckled. "Yeah, I've noticed. Beginning with the whole "baby daddy" exchange outside this very restaurant."

Relief flooded over me. He had laughed. Maybe this was going to be okay after all.

"I put all my patience and perseverance and trust into my career. I'm safe there. I get the results I want there, and it won't let me down. And being focused on work keeps all of those other thoughts away. Thoughts about my mother and my sister and how I've always felt like such a failure because of them."

"Ellie—"

I held up my hand. "I'm almost done. I meant that last sentence in the past tense. I have always *felt* like such a failure." I took in a deep breath, and let it out slowly. "You and Jasmine have shown me that maybe I need to start thinking about all of that differently. And maybe I need to start using some of my patience and perseverance in my personal life too." I laid my hands flat on the table. "Maybe not expect that everyone is going to let me down. And maybe I can count on myself in a relationship, too."

James sat up straighter in his chair, that hint of a smile still on his face.

"I am so sorry how I've treated you these past couple of days. I've been selfish and self-absorbed, and I took your patience and kindness for granted. It's been a couple of crazy weeks. Everything has changed and is going to keep changing in my life. But the best change has been you."

It was now, or never. "I don't have an official government form that I need you for any more. And I'm not even sure why you would stick around." I took in a big breath, and let it out slowly. "But I'm hoping you'll still be my boyfriend."

The smile on James's face got bigger. "I'm the best change in your life?"

"Without a doubt."

"Then I think we can try that," he said. "Let's see how it goes."

I shook my head. "Wait. Does that mean you're still my boyfriend? I can't tell."

James chuckled. "Yes, Ellie. I'm still your boyfriend."

I grinned in relief and took a big drink of my wine. I relaxed back in my chair. I hadn't realized I'd been sitting on the edge of my seat through our whole conversation.

"You know," I said. "This has all happened so fast with EB." I paused and looked at him. "I'm just figuring out now that I can be her family. Me. After everything that has happened, it has really hit home. Figuratively and literally. I want to be a home for EB. I want to have a home for her, and I think I've decided I want her to stay."

James's eyes went wide. "What made you decide that?"

"A couple of things. This talk, especially. But I was also trying to work on my Tate application, and I couldn't do it. In the middle of all of this, trying to win a prize seemed stupid. I don't need that award. I'm not even going to apply for it. Marks can have it."

"Wow," he laughed. "That's a surprise."

"I'll still publish the research so it can be used by other doctors, which is the important part. Besides, I can't stop thinking about what life was like for my sister and me when we were kids. We didn't have much luck. And I know foster care isn't always like that, but I can guarantee it won't be like that for EB if she stays with me. Permanently."

I surprised myself a little bit with that declaration. Permanently. Now that I'd said it out loud, my mind was flooded with a million things I needed to do—things I needed to learn—before EB moved in. First things first. When I talked to Mrs. Gonzalez, I needed to let her know that I didn't want to reapply to be a temporary foster parent, I wanted to care for EB. Permanently. She'd know what the next steps were.

I was so wrapped up in my own thoughts that I didn't even notice James was speaking.

"I'm sorry, James. I missed that. What did you say?"

"I said I think it's great that you're going to adopt EB."

I was taken aback. "Adopt? I didn't say I was going to adopt her, I said..." I trailed off. What, exactly, did I think I meant when I said I wanted to care for her permanently?

James just smiled and waited for me to get to the same conclusion he already had.

"You're right. That is what I'm saying. I want to adopt EB. Okay. That's big." I took another gulp of wine.

"It is big. That's what you want?" James asked me the question softly like he was trying not to scare me. Because yes, this was scary. After a moment, he reached across the table and took my fingers into his hand, and held them. Then he slowly leaned down and placed the lightest kiss upon the very tips. My stomach, which was already tightening at my new revelation, now tumbled over for a completely different reason.

"It is. Yes, it is." I laughed under my breath, and James gave my fingers a squeeze, let go, and slid his hand back to his side of the table. I missed his warmth immediately.

"Good for you. And EB, too. I can only imagine what she is going through, losing her mother at such a young age. You'll be great, Ellie. I know you will."

"Thank you. I hope so."

"I can help too. I mean, if you need me."

I knew that James's offer to help was exactly what I needed.

More than that, James himself, was exactly what I needed.
"I think we've already determined that I need you, James."
And this time, I was the one who reached across the table.

Chapter 35

- Ellie

I'd seen James a handful of times since my apology, but he'd been wrapped up in work the past week so we hadn't been together for a while. I ended up being on-call during that time, which was a good thing for me. It meant I was too busy to miss him.

I worked everything out with Mrs. Gonzalez so that my application to foster and then adopt EB was ready to go once the official "six week freeze" was over. She was very excited to hear I wanted to adopt—she was on my side.

She contacted me this morning and let me know that a temporary foster care provider had been found until my new application was approved. EB would be moving in with them shortly. I was anxious about the whole situation, but Mrs. Gonzalez assured me I would be happy with the home. And no, due to privacy rules she was not able to share that information with me at this time. I would, however, be allowed to meet EB with a *guardian ad litem* in a neutral setting, like a park, if I wanted. I couldn't wait to tell James about it.

Jasmine was as happy as James about the whole situation. When I brought her up to speed, I think her exact quote was, "Good. I knew you couldn't stay an idiot forever."

I had plans to meet James after work tonight, but I was a bit thrown when I got his text.

James: *I'm running late. Can you meet me at my parents' home rather than out?*

We hadn't talked a thing about me meeting his parents. Granted, I'd met his sister in the ER, delivering her baby, but that didn't even count. Neither one of us knew who the other was at that time. Meeting parents seemed like a big deal. Then again, everything with James had kind of been a big deal, so why not?

Me: Sure. Just let me know where and when.
James: *Make it 6:30. I should be able to make it by then.*
Me: Great. Do I need to bring anything?
James: *Nope.*
Me: Ok. See you then. Can't wait. By the way, I've got big news :)
James: *Me too :)*

Interesting. I wondered what his news was. I couldn't wait to surprise him with mine. And not only the news about getting to meet EB. I'd been working on some things, and he was going to be so happy. It was the least I could do for him, considering everything he had done for me.

James texted me his parents' address, and I headed out.

The drive took about 25 minutes, and I pulled up to a lovely two-story house with a big front yard. I knew I was in the right place because James's truck was there. There were quite a few cars parked in the driveway, in fact, and more on the street. It wasn't until I was out of my car and headed toward the house that I saw Jasmine's car. What on earth? What was Jasmine doing here? She and James barely knew each other.

I climbed the steps and reached to knock. James pulled the door open. "Hey, you made it." He leaned in for a quick kiss, then stepped back so I could come inside. He slipped his hand to the small of my back, and we entered the room.

"What is Jas—" I immediately stopped my question. "Mrs. Gonzalez? What are you doing here? And Marks?" *What on earth?* I turned back to James, who was still smiling. "What's going on?"

James's sister Lizzy rushed into the room, baby James in her arms. "Dr. Ellie. It's so good to finally meet you. Again. For real. I mean, nothing is more real than birthing a baby, but you know what I mean."

She came right over and gave me a one-armed hug, holding up her baby. "Look at him. Just look at him. Have you ever seen a more beautiful baby boy?" She was staring at her baby, then popped her head up. "Lie if you have to. I know you've seen a lot."

I burst out laughing. "He's beautiful. The most beautiful."

She beamed. "I thought so."

An older couple, who had been standing with Mrs. Gonzalez, walked over. "Ellie, I'd like you to meet my parents," James said.

"Mr. and Mrs. Cross. So nice to meet you." I held out my hand.

James's mother took my hand in both of hers. "I'm so glad to finally get to meet you, Ellie. We've heard so much about you."

James's dad did the same, taking my hand in both of his. "Please. Call us Marge and Bill."

When Bill stepped back, I saw Marks take a step closer to Jasmine, sliding his arm around her waist. And then she leaned her head against his shoulder. Okay, I really did not know what was going on.

Mrs. Gonzalez gave me a little wave from across the room, and once again I turned to James. "You've got to tell me. What is going on?"

He laughed and took my hand. "It's a good thing. You know how Mrs. Gonzalez told you a temporary home was found for EB?"

I turned towards Mrs. Gonzalez, and back to James. "Yes. But why do you know? I thought that information was private."

"It is. Unless you're the temporary home," said Mrs. Gonzalez.

I whipped my head back to Mrs. Gonzalez, who smiled at me. Big. "I couldn't tell you," Mrs. Gonzalez said, "But they can."

My mind was going a million miles a minute, jumping to a ton of conclusions. "Um, I don't think I understand. I need some help."

Jasmine laughed out loud. "Look at you. Asking for help. So much has changed in such a short time."

I squinted my eyes at Jasmine, and she and Marks both grinned.

Mrs. Cross—Marge—spoke up. "James told us everything that was going on with EB, especially how concerned you were about where she would end up during your application freeze." I could feel heat rise to my face. That was going to be a sore spot for some time.

"We met with Mrs. Gonzalez last week, and since they are always in need of foster families, and this was a special situation, she was able to push our application through."

My heart raced, and I bit my tongue, not wanting to blurt out what I thought was happening, in case I was wrong. "What was the special situation?" I asked Mrs. Gonzalez.

"We had a relation to the child make a mistake on her application. We couldn't unfreeze her application, but we discussed that error with the judge. It was especially persuasive when I asked him to speed up the approval for the Cross's, since they've been foster parents before, and are still in the system."

"What? You have?" My mind was racing. I looked at James.

"My parents fostered when my younger brothers were in high school. You'll get to meet those clowns soon enough."

"You have foster brothers? You never told me." I was shocked.

"I know. But whenever we talked about fostering, you were usually pretty upset. I was mostly trying to get you through it. I think you'll agree, there was never a right time."

I nodded. He was right.

Mr. Cross joined in. "We're going to foster EB until your application is approved. She'll be moving in with us in two days, and you can come and visit and stay anytime you want."

What I thought was happening was happening. I wasn't wrong. Tears welled in my eyes. It seemed like everyone in the room was holding their breath, waiting.

"You did this for me? And for EB?" I tried to hold back the tears, but I felt the first one drop.

"We did," said the Crosses.

"We did," said Lizzy from the sofa.

"We did," said Mrs. Gonzalez.

I looked at James. He still had one of my hands in his.

"I did," he said softly, holding my gaze.

Without missing a beat, I jumped in his arms. He laughed, took a step backward, then regained his footing.

"Thank you. Thank you. How will I ever thank you?" I was laughing and crying and couldn't seem to catch my breath. The whole room was laughing with me.

James whispered in my ear. "I'm sure we can come up with something."

I laughed and kissed him. I'm sure we could come up with something, too.

After a couple of hours of visiting and eating—no surprise, Mrs. Cross was as good of a cook as James was—the party started to break up. Before they could get away, I finally cornered Jasmine and Marks and laughed out loud when I found out they had recently begun dating. They laughed along with me. They genuinely seemed happy.

Turns out Marks had even given me another reference to use for my adoption application. That application was much more complex than the fostering application, and I was going to need a lot more references than just James and Jasmine. I'd been wrong about so many things—maybe I'd been wrong about Marks, too?

I couldn't wait for Jasmine to tell me all about how the two of them got together. I could hardly believe it.

Lizzy went to bed with the baby, and Marge and Bill went to watch TV. James and I were still in the front room, sitting on the sofa.

I had my head on his shoulder with one leg draped over his, and his arm was around me, holding me close. It had been a long, exciting day, and I was beat.

"I can't believe EB is going to be here in two days. I can't wait to meet her," I said.

"I know. We'll have it all figured out, so you can be here when she gets here. She'll know from the beginning that it's you she's going to end up with."

I could only smile, thinking about it.

"So what was the big news?" James asked, running small circles around my shoulder. "You said in your text you had big news to tell me, too."

I sat up straight. "You're right. I do. I forgot all about it." I turned to James on the sofa.

"I looked into the rules and regulations for bidding on the new children's wing. It is pretty strict. But after asking around, I found out that I can introduce you to members of the board who make the final decision."

"Really?"

"Yep. There's a golfing event next weekend, and I'm sure several of them will be there. It'll be the perfect place to meet. We can play, and I'll introduce you around."

"You play golf?" he asked.

"No. But I figured you did."

He just looked at me.

"You don't?" I asked.

"I don't," he said.

I started laughing, and couldn't stop. It didn't take long until James was laughing too.

"You're going to have to explain what's so funny," he said. He reached out and took my hand.

"When I saw you at the Hospital Charity Ball, with your tanned skin and sun-bleached hair, I was sure you were some rich jerk who played golf all day."

"As opposed to a self-made man who worked hard at an outdoor job?"

"Exactly opposed to that."

He shook his head. "I said this to you the first time we met. Careful about making assumptions. They can make an as—"

I didn't let him finish. I stopped him with a kiss.

By the way he kissed me back, I'm pretty sure he was okay with that.

Epilogue

I hated that it was time to go, but I needed to get back to my place. I had a full day of patients tomorrow, and it was late. James took my hand, and we walked outside.

"I still can't believe everything you guys are doing for EB and me. I will never get over it." I ran my thumb over James's wrist. I didn't want this night to end.

"You don't need to get over it, you just need to—" James stopped in his tracks.

He turned and faced me full-on.

"This is your car?" he asked.

"Yeah...? Why? Do I have a flat or something?" I dropped James's hand and moved to my car. I looked at the tires and moved around to the other side.

James ran his hand down his face. "Nope. No flat. But turns out there *is* something you'll need to get over."

Now I was just confused. "What are you talking about?"

James chuckled, and he had a look on his face that I'd never seen before.

"What's going on?" I asked.

"You are not going to believe this. I don't believe it." He walked over and glanced into the window of my car. "You know the night you delivered baby James?"

"Of course I do. I'll never forget it." That night was burned in my memory.

"I know a lot happened that night. But think about it for a second."

"Ok," I said. "There was the charity ball. You spilling drinks all over me. Me rushing to the hosp—. My car! My car was stolen that night. I mean, weirdly stolen. And returned. What do you know about—"

James's eyes were big, and his eyebrows were raised. His hands—those beautiful hands—were stuffed in his front pockets. He didn't say a word.

It took me a minute, but I got it.

"You? You stole my car?"

He paused. "I like to think that I borrowed your car."

"I bet you like to think that." I started to laugh. "Oh my gosh, it was you." By now James was laughing too.

"It was an emergency. I had to get to the hospital, You can see how—"

"Oh, I can see alright."

James took me in his arms, holding me close. "Tell me. What can I do? What can I do to make it up to you?"

I hugged him closer, and whispered in his ear, "I'm sure we can come up with something."

Two Days Later
- Ellie

Internally, I was kind of a wreck. I could absolutely keep my cool in the hospital, but after everything I'd gone through with my sister, losing her in foster care, losing her when we had our falling out, then losing her forever when she died, I was finally going to meet her daughter.

EB. My niece. Who just might be *my* daughter someday. Emotional barely began to describe how I was feeling.

I was sitting in the Cross's living room with James, waiting for Mrs. Gonzalez and EB to arrive. I wasn't pacing, but that was only because James had such a tight grip on my hand, I couldn't move. Plus, I didn't want to make anyone else more nervous watching me walk around.

We all heard it. A car pulled into the driveway. Everyone stood up. I smoothed my damp hands down the front of my jeans. We'd decided we didn't want to overwhelm EB, so Lizzy was in the family room with baby James, and Mr. and Mrs. Cross went out to greet her first. Now I started pacing.

I could hear introductions being made, and I waited for what seemed like an eternity. Mrs. Gonzalez walked in, with a slight, thin girl, not far behind. Wavy, brown hair to her shoulders with big brown eyes. She could have been my sister, from so many years ago.

"EB," Mrs. Gonzalez said, "I want you to meet your Aunt Ellie."

I approached and crouched down on one knee. "Hi EB. It's so good to meet you." I swiped a tear away from my cheek. "I'm so sorry about your mom."

Tears welled in her eyes, but they didn't fall.

"I know nothing can take her place, but we want to be here for you. We're going to be here for you any way that we can."

It took just one beat. The tears fell. And then she threw herself in my arms.

It was okay. We were going to be okay.

I didn't think it would be easy, and I knew EB and I would

have a lot of getting to know each other and growing to-gether to do, but we were going to be okay.

Two Months Later
- *Ellie*

James was hosting a cookout at his house. We wanted EB to meet more of our friends. She was living with me now, and we thought she had adjusted enough to expand beyond family. They were almost all here, including Lizzy's husband Theo, whom I'd just met for the first time. Lizzy was thrilled to have him home, and he was besotted with his new baby.

Lizzy and Theo were talking with some old friends who hadn't seen Theo since before his deployment. James's parents were sitting with EB, who was holding baby James. He was growing like a weed, smiling and cooing. And you could already tell he was going to be a big boy like his dad and his namesake.

Having baby James to help care for was a blessing in disguise for EB. It seemed to distract her and help take her out of her own problems. And who didn't love a sweet baby? She was adjusting, though of course there were good days and bad. But we were working through it. Together.

James's brothers were all supposed to show up at some point, but they were hard to nail down. Max was out of town, which seemed to be the case every weekend, but he said he'd try to make it back, and Taylor and Tyler, the twins, were being downright vague. I'd only met each of them a couple of times over the past two months. I loved how everyone in the family referred to them as brothers, even though Taylor and Tyler were the boys they fostered, and they had another family of their own. It reinforced for me how loving and giving James's family was, and how there were a lot of ways to create a family.

Jasmine was on her way over, and Marks was coming later. Their romance had fizzled as quickly as it started, having decided they were better off as friends. If you could believe it, even I was warming up to the guy. He found out last week he won the Tate, and I was actually happy for him. I couldn't believe how much it didn't matter to me anymore. But I was still glad he and Jasmine weren't dating—he wasn't good enough for her.

"I know you guys have been really busy, but we still haven't had that after-the-cooking-class-cooking-class you were going to host," Brett said, walking up. He had cold beers in his hand for both Shauna and me.

Shauna wrapped her hand around the beer. "Thanks, babe. That's right. If I remember correctly—and I do—we won the cook-off." She took a swallow of beer and gave James and me a big grin.

James flipped over the burgers and moved the hot dogs aside. "You're right. We need to do that. It's definitely going to be different from what we planned, but everything is different now."

He smiled at me, and I leaned in and gave him a quick kiss. "Do you guys think that Chef Mike really expected couples to come out of his *Lonely Hearts Club Cooking Class*?"

Shauna and Brett looked at each other, then back to us. "I don't know," Shauna said and grinned. "But it worked."

Brett motioned to the yard. "He's not here?"

"He and his wife are looking into another restaurant location today, so they couldn't make it." James picked up his beer and took a drink. "You all need to meet his wife."

"I haven't met her, yet," I said, "but I'm guessing she's great if his matchmaking skills for himself were as good as what he did for us."

I held up my bottle. "A Toast. To Chef Mike." And everyone joined in.

One Year Later
- James

We were back where it had all started. The Annual Merit Memorial Hospital Charity Ball. I was a sponsor this year, making sure that everyone knew about my home construction business.

'Cross Construction - Where Every Home Has a Story to Tell.'

I decided not to get into commercial building after all. With everything that had happened with Ellie and EB over the past year, family was where my heart was. And helping people build the home of their dreams, helping them build their families—that was where I wanted to be. Like what Ellie did—but different.

"Did you guys see that Chef Mike is offering your cooking class again?" Jasmine asked. "But it looks like it's in a different location." She had walked up to us after looking at all of the silent auction items.

"It is. He expanded. It's north of the city, out a little bit. NoBo. Short for Northbound, just like SoBo and Southbound. Same amazing food." I'd taken Ellie and EB there when it first opened. We'd follow Chef Mike anywhere.

"It's a great place. You should check it out. Did you decide to bid on anything?" Ellie asked.

"There were definitely some cool things," Jasmine replied. "I'm thinking about one of the tropical vacation trips."

I made big don't-talk-about-that eyes at Jasmine, which she picked up on.

"Or I don't know," she said. "There are some gorgeous custom jewelry pieces, too. Come on, I'll show you."

Ellie smiled at me. "Be right back."

I watched them walk away. I had bid on two of the tropical trips for two. The worst thing that would happen is I'd win them both. Which wouldn't be bad. It was for a good cause.

I was getting a little ahead of myself with the auction items, but I wasn't worried. Tonight was the big night. I was proposing to Ellie. And one of those trips would be perfect for our honeymoon. I'd wanted to ask her for months, but I also wanted to give both her and EB time to get to know each other on their own. I decided I'd waited long enough.

EB was staying with my parents tonight, and she would love every minute of it. They spoiled her. But not rotten. She could never be rotten. When people heard her story, sometimes they would comment on how lucky she was. But they were wrong. We were the lucky ones—to have her in our lives.

And who knows, maybe we'd all get lucky again, and EB would end up with a sibling or two.

One thing I did know...we were sure going to try.

Now I just had to go get my girl and get out of here.

- Jasmine

"Hey, Jasmine, we're going to head out. Are you going to stay?" Ellie asked.

I immediately glanced over to where Quinn—Cowboy Quinn, as he had become in my mind—was talking to Chef Mike. I could feel my eyes get small and squinty. What was up with him anyway?

I straightened my spine. "I think I'll leave now, too."

Ellie's head turned to see where I'd looked, and she couldn't keep her smile off her face. "Maybe you should say goodbye to Quinn before we go. I like him for you."

I scoffed. "How could you? You met him for like, one second. I only met him for two."

"I don't know, it just seemed when you were with him, you had your spark back."

She wasn't wrong. The few moments Quinn and I spoke were electric. And it was the first time in a while that I felt like myself. Like I wasn't forcing something.

I shook my head to clear my thoughts.

"That wasn't about Quinn. That was just this night. You know how much I like a party."

I could tell Ellie wasn't buying it, but she just gave me a little nod.

"Besides," I said. "He's some kind of farm boy, and I'm a city girl. I'll never see him again." I set my drink down on the table. "Come on. I'll walk out with you and James."

- Ellie

We were on our way to pick up EB after the ball, and James just drove right past our exit.

"Hey, you missed the exit," I said. I turned my head to James. EB was at his parent's house, and we were supposed to be picking her up..

"Oh, sorry. I told my mom I'd bring over that bookshelf for her to use in EB's room, and I forgot to bring it when we dropped her off. I thought I'd grab it first." He glanced at me. "And you can come in and get a slice of pizza."

I scrunched up my forehead. I *was* hungry. "It's late, but yeah, pizza sounds good right now."

James reached across the console and took my hand in his. "I know my girl."

I laughed. "Yes, you do."

We pulled into James's driveway, and he came around and opened my door, then helped me out of the truck. He took my hand and said, "Can you believe it's only been a year since we met?"

I shook my head. "No, not with everything that has happened. You, EB, your family."

We walked up the steps, and James pulled open the door. I was a bit distracted, thinking about the past year, and didn't notice when he stepped into the house before me. A little odd—James was a perfect gentleman, and always opened and held doors for me.

I walked into the house, and...I took it in all at once.

There were little electric candle lights everywhere. Scattered on the hearth, across the mantle, on the side tables, and gathered in clusters on the floor. The room was glowing with the most beautiful golden light.

There was music playing softly in the background, and there were fresh bouquets of flowers on the tabletops. And James. James was on one knee in front of me.

My hands flew to my mouth, and I blurted out, "I thought we were getting pizza."

And James smiled.

"We fell in love over food," he said. "It seems only right that we're talking about it now." He tilted his head. "You want me to get you something to eat first?"

I shook my head slowly, my hands still covering my mouth.

"Okay, then," He nodded his head, and cleared his throat.

"Ellie, you were the biggest surprise of my life, and now you're the biggest love of my life. I don't want another day to go by without you and EB permanently in my life."

James raised up his hands and opened a little black box. The cushion-cut diamond reflected off the candles and threw off prisms of light, showering the room in tiny rainbows.

"You're the most beautiful, intelligent, strongest woman I know, and you are a fantastic mom. And I love you, with all my heart. Will you do me the honor and marry me?"

I placed my hand into James's hand and knelt down beside him. He pulled the ring out of the box, and I nodded and nodded, and he slipped the ring onto my finger. Tears streamed down my face. I was speechless.

"Good," he said. "Because I only want to do this with you," he slipped his hand into his pocket and pulled out another ring box, "and EB."

He opened the box and inside was a small, gold ring with an infinity design, with three small diamonds clustered in the middle.

"The three diamonds are for you, EB, and me. And the infinity sign is for how long I will love you both."

I threw my arms around James, and we toppled over onto the floor. "Yes, yes!" I cried.

We were both laughing, and I was crying, and I kissed James all over his face. And I'm pretty sure he had a couple of tears sparkling in his eyes, too.

We sat up and pushed over to the wall, then leaned up against it. I held out my hand to admire the ring.

"I love it, James. It's perfect." I leaned over and kissed him "You're perfect, too. I love you."

We sat there, holding hands, and let the soft music play. The lights flickered, and we enjoyed the moment.

A year ago. It was just a year ago. I had been all alone, except for Jasmine. And now I had EB, and James, and his family, and new friends...

I couldn't wait to see what the next year would bring.

XOX

Don't Want to See Things End with Ellie and James?

How about an exclusive scene four years into their future? James is up to some of his old tricks and you don't want to miss it!
*Get instant access to an **exclusive bonus scene** delivered straight to your inbox by visiting my site listed below or scanning the QR code!*
https://www.subscribepage.com/x9z1h6

Remember Ellie's best friend Jasmine? Things don't turn out quite like she thought they would, and running into Cowboy Quinn again - literally! – is just the beginning.
Turn the page and keep reading *for a sneak peek into the first chapters of her book!*
Preorder Jasmine's story - Anything I Can Do by Mary Carson on Amazon or
Scan the QR code on the next page with your phone camera and get whisked away to pre-order on Amazon.
Turn the page and keep reading for Jasmine's story.

Scan the QR code above with your phone camera and get whisked away to pre-order on Amazon.

Keep reading for Jasmine's story.

Anything I Can Do

An opposites attract, forced proximity (kinda?), small town romance

- *Jasmine*

I love a party. I love the energy, the excitement, all of the different people—even when it's kind of against my free will—like tonight—I still love a party.

A server walked by, and I snagged a glass of champagne. My best friend, Ellie, and her boyfriend (soon-to-be-fiance—*shh, don't tell anyone*) James, were across the room, talking to Chef Mike, whom I'd met on several occasions at his restaurants around town, and I was itching to join their conversation. Instead, I was mixing and mingling, meeting new people, making sure they knew about my family's business, and how to be a part of it.

The room was filled with people, and there was an excited buzz in the air. We were at the Sponsor's Pre-party Cocktail Hour for the annual Merit Memorial Hospital Charity Ball.

As the title suggested, everyone here had sponsored tonight's event, so they were at least in some way used to giving their money away. I was here to convince them to give it to me. Or more accurately, give it to my family's medical research business, Kaling Medical. Not that I was a part of the business. I was a nurse at Merit Memorial.

"Right now they're working on a new device and procedure to help limit the damage caused by stroke," I said, and took a quick swallow of my drink. I refocused on the woman I was speaking with, Denise Wilson. She owned several yoga studios in the area. I introduced myself after complimenting her fabulous necklace. It was a multi-layered strand of various-sized beads, all in the green and blue colors of the ocean. Telling her how much I liked it was the perfect way to open up a conversation.

Denise nodded her head. "Strokes just seem to come out of nowhere and they can be devastating. It's amazing that you're involved in that kind of work."

"Oh no. I hope that doesn't mean you've experienced it first hand?" It could be tricky talking about medical issues because you didn't know who had experienced what. But when you're in the biz, and literally at a hospital event, you could guarantee there was going to be a lot of medical talk.

"Not personally, no, thank goodness. But it's a real fear, especially as my parents are getting older. Stroke, heart attack. You don't know what might happen." She took a sip of her drink. "I'm not a big worrier, but I am aware."

"Are they involved at all in your yoga practice? I have to believe that can only help them." It was so easy to mingle. You just asked questions, and let the other person talk. Simple. Plus, I genuinely liked meeting new people. So even though I'm not actually an employee of my family's business, attending events on their behalf was one of the few things I was willing to do for them. Sometimes grudgingly, but still.

"Yes. It took them years, but they both do yoga twice a week. Now if I could only get them to eat better."

"Oh! Have you met Chef Mike? Let me introduce you. He does a lot of innovative things with food and events and catering. Maybe he'll have some ideas for you."

We made our way towards the other side of the room, where Chef Mike and my friends had been moments before. This small room, which was off to the side of the ballroom where the charity ball would be held, had gotten much more crowded in that short amount of time. Since I barely broke 5'5" even in my heels, I couldn't see my friends.

Chef Mike was a big guy, like linebacker big, so I spotted him first, and then some people shifted out of our way. I was looking for Ellie and James, but hellooo there, tall, dark, and handsome. Where did you come from?

Okay, he wasn't that tall. I didn't think he was six feet, but everyone was taller than me. He was dark; dark hair, dark eyes, dark skin. And he was most definitely handsome. I was sticking with it—tall, dark, and handsome.

"Chef Mike. Hi. I hope you don't mind if we interrupt." Chef Mike was a funny, gregarious guy. He wouldn't mind the interruption. James and Ellie were nowhere to be seen.

"Jasmine. Hi." He leaned way down and gave me a hug. "What a nice surprise. Are you here with Ellie and James?" Chef Mike's cooking class—he auctioned it off every year at the charity ball—was actually how Ellie and James met. It was a singles event called "Sgt. Pepper's Lonely Hearts Club Cooking Class." It had been known to match up a couple or two.

"Not tonight. Tonight I'm here for my family's business. I wanted you to meet Denise. She owns several yoga studios in town. I told her you might have some ideas on helping her get her parents to start eating healthier." Chef Mike reached out and shook Denise's hand.

"Nice to meet you. And perfect timing. We were just discussing healthier eating. Jasmine. Denise. This is Quinn O'Connell, of O'Connell Organics."

Denise and Quinn shook hands, and then Chef Mike immediately began discussing the food habits of Denise's parents. I turned to shake Quinn's hand, and I enjoyed the fact that he was even more handsome closeup. It was fun for me.

What was *not* fun for me? When his lopsided smile and his firm handshake sent a brief tingle of electricity up my arm. Shoot. Finding this guy attractive was one thing. Actually being attracted was something else. I didn't want to be attracted. Even to tall, dark, and handsome.

I needed to distract myself.

"Would I know O'Connell Organics from anywhere?" I asked.

"You might. Our biggest presence right now is at farmers markets."

"Hmm." I tapped my lower lip. "I can't remember the last time I was at a farmers market."

"What about farm-to-table restaurants?" he asked.

"Wait. Did you just say 'charmed and fables?'"

"What? No. Why would I say that?"

"I don't know, but if we're talking about fairy tales, I always thought I should be a princess, and if your organic food can make that happen, I'm here for it."

Quinn gave me a look like he wasn't so sure about me.

"So you're not a princess," Quinn said, deadpan.

"Not yet. But now that I'm thinking about it, the charmed part you mentioned is usually about the guy. I don't need some new twist on prince charming, or a white knight riding up on his horse like some modern-day cowboy to save me. I'm perfectly capable of saving myself."

"I never said anything about being charmed. Or fabled, for that matter. You did. And what do you have against cowboys?"

"Nothing," I said, puzzled. "Who doesn't like a cowboy?"

"I thought you didn't." He gave his head a little shake. "Let's try again. I said farm. To. Table."

"Ohhhh." I dragged it out a bit. "Sorry, the last time I did anything memorable with a table it was dancing on it, and it had nothing to do with organic food."

This time, I didn't get the look, I got the laugh. Perfect.

Quinn was smiling that crooked smile again. "What about you?" he asked. "You said you're here for your family's business. What do you do?"

This didn't seem to be the right time—or even a necessary time—to go into the whole "I'm here for my family's business but I'm not actually part of it" thing—so I gave him the basics.

"That's really important work," he said.

I cocked my head to the side. "Why does that sound like the right words to say, and yet I don't get the feeling you actually mean them."

"What? No. I—"

The director of the event tapped a spoon against a champagne flute, gathering everyone's attention. "Ladies and gentlemen, thank you again for being sponsors for our ball tonight. I hope you have enjoyed your happy hour. We wanted to let you know that the ballroom next door is now open. Enjoy the rest of your evening, and thank you again."

I turned to Quinn. "Quinn. It was nice meeting you. Enjoy the rest of your night." I gave a little wave to Denise and Chef Mike and made my way to the ballroom. My official work for the night was done, so I was going to find Ellie and James.

I was glad my interaction with Quinn O'Connell didn't turn into some fabulously flirtatious thing. He seemed more confused by me than anything. Plus, that lack of flirtation was proof that I could ignore that little thrill I got when we shook hands. It was proof that I wasn't interested.

Because the truth was, I wasn't interested in being interested in anyone right now.

"But will she like it?"

"You know she loves anything you do with her," Ellie said.

"I know, but I feel like I should try to expand her horizons."

"It probably wouldn't be a bad time to expand your own horizons." Ellie, or Dr. Eleanor Dumont, as she was known around here, bumped her shoulder into mine.

I let out a deep breath and took a drink of my champagne. "You're not wrong."

We were standing in front of one of the silent auction items. The ballroom was glittering, throwing slivers of light over everything. The low lighting and the reflective crystals from the chandeliers reminded me of what I wore to last year's event. No crystal bustier for me this year. I was all business, even in formal wear. Black, black, and more black. Tailored and a bit severe, but still beautiful. Only one large bracelet cuff of crystals. I couldn't completely shut off who I was, even when I was representing my family's business.

"A trail ride on horseback is so far outside my world," I said, "I won't just be expanding my horizons, I think it might put me in a new galaxy, far, far away."

"Again. Might not be the worst thing for you. You seem to be in a bit of a slump lately, and that's not like you. Plus, EB will love it no matter what. 'Cause it's with you."

EB was Ellie's niece, soon to be adopted daughter. We all fell in love with her when Ellie started taking care of her after Ellie's sister died. She was a funny, clever, eight-year-old with a soft heart. I tried to spoil her when I could.

"I don't know if I'd call it a slump, exactly. It's not like I don't have guys to date. I do. Lots of guys." I tried to muster up some enthusiasm, but Ellie was right. I was in a slump, no matter how much I tried to deny it.

I grabbed the pen and jotted down my bid. On top of a horse was the exact opposite of down in the dumps. Maybe it would work.

"Come on. Let's see what else we can find. If getting you in a saddle isn't going to do it for you, maybe we can—"

Ellie didn't finish her sentence, because she was interrupted. By Quinn O'Connell.

"Getting back in the saddle cures a lot of things. I bet it can cure you, too." He smiled right at me, then at Ellie.

"I beg your pardon? Cure me of what, exactly?" I crossed my arms over my chest. Ellie's eyebrows were raised practically to her forehead, and she looked from me to Quinn, then back to me.

"I'm not sure, exactly, but it works wonders. I'm sure it can help," he said.

"And how would you know?"

"I'm Farm Boy Ranch."

"You're what?"

"Farm Boy Ranch. The ranch offering the trail rides you just bid on."

"You're Farm Boy Ranch?" It was a question, but I said it more like a statement.

"Yes."

"And O'Connell Organics."

"Yes."

"And a cowboy."

"Also. Yes."

"Jasmine, were you going to introduce me to your friend?" Ellie's eyebrows were still raised, and she had a slight smile on her face.

"I'd like to meet your friend, too, Jasmine." And though I knew he wasn't trying to, my ex-boyfriend—now just friend—Dr. John Marks suddenly materialized by my side, sounding a bit on the jealous side. Not what I needed right now.

"You guys. He's not really a fr—"

"Nice to meet you both." Quinn reached out his hand to shake first Marks' hand, then Ellie's. They introduced themselves. And I was reminded of that little spark from our earlier handshake.

"I'm Quinn O'Connell, with Farm Boy Ranch and O'Connell Organics. Jasmine and I met earlier, and after she wins the horseback ride, I'll be seeing more of her. Maybe you guys can join her." He flashed them both that lopsided smile and turned back to me. "I need to meet with some other people. I'll see you around." Quinn took a step away and then winked at me.

He *winked* at me. What. On. Earth?

"What was that all about?" Ellie asked.

She still had her eyebrows raised. I think they might have frozen that way.

"Yeah, I'd like to know too." Marks had a slight scowl on his face.

"It's nothing. I barely know him."

"I don't like him."

"Marks, you haven't liked a single guy I've gone out with since we broke up. And I'm not even going out with this guy." I was completely exasperated.

"Can you blame me?" he retorted.

Marks was a decent enough guy, once you got past his ego. But we found out pretty quickly we had absolutely nothing in common but work. I had enough of work as Nurse Manager of Labor and Delivery and my on-call shifts—I didn't need to relive it all on my time off, too.

"You know we're better off as friends," I said.

"I know. I still don't like him." He continued to scowl. "I'm going to get a drink. Can I get you guys anything?"

Ellie held up her almost empty champagne glass and nodded. I shook my head.

"I'll be right back. Don't start dating that guy in the meantime." He walked away.

"What the—?"

I called after him. "I don't even like him. I'm not going out with him."

Marks just kept walking, not acknowledging me at all.

I turned to Ellie and threw my hands up in the air.

She tossed back the last of her champagne and gave me a sly smile.

Then she said one word.

"Yet."

Don't miss out on what happens next. Want this book delivered directly to your reading device when it releases? Pre-order it now on Amazon at Anything I Can Do by Mary Carson. Or scan the QR code below to be whisked away to Amazon!

Acknowledgments

When I sat down to write this book, I thought I was done when I typed 'the end.' But then I decided to *publish* a book, and there was a second draft that I needed to write, and then a third, then edits, then more edits, and more and more and more, and I was sure I would *never* be done.

You want to know when I finally knew I was done with my book? When I sat down to write *this*, the acknowledgements. That's when I knew I had really done it.

It's surreal to be writing this. Because good golly, it means I wrote a book!

And I had *tons* of help along the way.

My greatest of thanks goes to:

Susan Kostelecky. You were my biggest cheerleader, word by word, chapter by chapter. Every time you said you couldn't wait for the next chapter it encouraged me to write the next. I couldn't have done it without you.

My mom and dad, my girls, my incredible family of siblings and in-laws, and my nieces and nephews. Having a family of voracious readers was priceless in the development of this story. I can't thank you enough for your kind and funny feedback, suggestions, and encouragement throughout the writing (and rewriting!) of this book.

Kaylan Sharp of BabyMamaco.com. You are incredible at what you do, and I can't thank you enough for sharing your expertise on baby delivery and obstetrics, and for reading and rereading until I got it right. Babies – and their mamas! – are lucky to have you! (And any inaccuracies are entirely my own.)

Melanie Harlow. How can I thank you enough? Your mentorship group is like nothing else out there, and I will be forever grateful for the knowledge and wisdom you have so generously (and often, hilariously) shared. Thank you.

My first little writing group. T, trash it or treasure it will go down in the books. And **Anise Rae**, that "-ing" trick you taught me as you went through my book was worth a thousand rewrites. *Thank you for everything!*

My second little writing group. Cate Lane and Julia Connors - thank you both for sharing everything you went through before I went through it. I am so grateful I didn't have to do it alone.

My ARC readers, Launch Team, and friends near and far. For taking a chance on a brand new author, and sharing your thoughts with anyone who would listen. I can't thank you enough.

And if you're still with me...thank you **to *you*.** For spending your precious time reading this. I hope you loved Ellie and James as much as I did. And lastly,

Mr. Carson. You make me feel like I can do anything because you make anything possible.

About the Author

Mary Carson likes her chocolate salted and her romance sweet.

She writes sweet romance with a kiss, and you won't be embarrassed to gift her books to your mom.

When Mary isn't reading or writing, she's enjoying the lake in North Carolina with her very big family and even bigger group of friends. *You never know just how many friends you have until you have a lake house.*

Keep in touch with Mary through social media or through her newsletter with the links below- she promises to only send the good stuff.

www.MaryCarsonBooks.com

instagram.com/marycarsonbooks

facebook.com/Mary-Carson-Author-106007625470515

amazon.com/Mary-Carson/e/B0B138V1RF

Made in the USA
Coppell, TX
03 October 2022